James Currie, William Pitt

A Letter, Commercial and Political, Addressed to the Rt. Honble. William Pitt

in which the real interests of Britain, in the present crisis, are considered,

and some observations are offered on the general state of Europe

James Currie, William Pitt

A Letter, Commercial and Political, Addressed to the Rt. Honble. William Pitt
*in which the real interests of Britain, in the present crisis, are considered, and some
observations are offered on the general state of Europe*

ISBN/EAN: 9783337380953

Printed in Europe, USA, Canada, Australia, Japan

Cover: Foto ©Andreas Hilbeck / pixelio.de

More available books at **www.hansebooks.com**

A

LETTER,

RCIAL AND POLITICAL,

ADDRESSED TO

H^{onble}. WILLIAM PITT:

IN WHICH

TERESTS OF B

IN THE

SENT CRISI

RE CONSIDERED,

AND

VATIONS ARE

ON THE

ERAL STATE

UROPE.

ITION, CORRECTED

PER WILSO

COUNSEL AGAINS
TS ARE PRINCE
OF THE EARTH

LONDON:

PRINTED   AND J. ROBINSON

MDCCXCIII.

e Shilling and S

PREFACE.

THE following Letter was originally written, as well as printed, in so hasty a manner, that some inaccuracies of composition escaped notice, as well as several errors of the press—it was perceived too, on a farther review, that some illustrations and additions to particular passages were wanted, and a short, but general summary of the whole.—Such corrections and enlargements have accordingly been made; a Postscript has been added, exemplifying, in some of the more material points, the application of events subsequent to the original publication of the Letter, to the representations and reasonings it contains; and the whole, it is hoped, will now be found less unworthy of the favourable reception which the first edition has met with.

SIR,

AN inquiry into the caufes of the general calamities which affect the commercial and manufacturing interefts, and the connexion which thefe may have with the meafures of government, feems properly addreffed to you as the Minifter of the Crown, and the Leader of the Houfe of Commons.

A concurrence of fortune and talents has raifed you to a degree of confequence in the public eye which no other individual of the age has attained, and your friends having afcribed to you much of our late unexampled profperity, your enemies will doubtlefs impute to you our prefent unparalleled diftrefs. Party zeal may blind the one and the other; but the fubject of the prefent inquiry muft in every point of view prefs with peculiar force on your mind.

The writer of this was one of the warmeft of your admirers. The progrefs of time and of events has cooled his enthufiafm refpecting you, but has not, as is often the cafe, turned it into hoftility. Neither difpofed to offend or flatter, he would deliver his fentiments with the deference due to

B   your

your extraordinary talents, but with the earneſtneſs and ſolemnity ſuited to the preſent criſis of human affairs.

That the calamities which affect our commerce and manufactures are great beyond example, it is unneceſſary to prove. The unprecedented and alarming meaſures which are reſorted to in parliament to prevent the univerſal wreck of credit, put this beyond a doubt.—It does not however ſeem to be generally obſerved that theſe calamities are not peculiar to Britain. Bankruptcies have ſpread and are ſpreading every where over the continent of Europe, through France, Holland, Germany, Poland, Ruſſia, Italy, and Spain, and every where private as well as public credit is impaired or deſtroyed. If the injury to commerce and manufactures be more felt in Britain than elſewhere, it is becauſe we have had more commerce and manufactures to be injured. And this reaſon, which explains why Britain ſuffers apparently more than the other kingdoms of Europe, will alſo explain why the different towns and counties of Britain ſuffer at preſent exactly in proportion to their former commercial proſperity. In one reſpect England differs at this juncture from moſt of the other European nations—our public credit is yet tolerably ſound—Whilſt the governments of Ruſſia, Auſtria, Poland, France, and Spain, are either bankrupt, or on the verge of bankruptcy, and have had recourſe to practices that differ little from open rapine.

I ſtate theſe facts on authorities to ſome of which I ſhall allude as I go on, but I believe that you will admit them at once as unqueſtionable.

To ſeek for the origin of ſuch general calamities within the precincts of a ſingle kingdom, is to labour to no purpoſe. They are to be traced, as it appears, to the prevalence and extenſion of the war-ſyſtem throughout Europe, ſupported as it has been by the univerſal adoption of the funding-ſyſtem. As this idea has not been laid before the public, as perhaps

haps it may not have prefented itfelf fully even to your mind, and as it feems to be of the utmoft importance, I muft beg leave to unfold it at fome length, and to fhew its application to our own diftreffes.

Speculative men, Sir, in the retirement of their clofets, have delighted to contemplate the progrefs of knowledge, and to fhew its happy effects on the condition of our fpecies. The truth feems to be, as was afferted by Lord Bacon, that " knowledge is power," or, to fpeak more popularly, that power is increafed in proportion to knowledge. But the effects of power on human happinefs depend on the wifdom and benevolence by which it is directed; and where thefe are not found in a correfponding degree, an increafe of power muft often add to the miferies of the human race. Without however difputing the happy influences of the progrefs of knowledge on the whole, it may be doubted whether thefe have extended in any confiderable degree to the general political fyftem; and it may be clearly fhewn, that its effects on the intercourfe of nations with each other, have been hitherto in many refpects injurious.

Among favages the means of intercourfe are reftricted to tribes who are neighbours, and hoftilities are confined in the fame manner. As knowledge increafes, thefe means are multiplied and extended, and nations not in immediate vicinity learn to mingle in each other's affairs. This is abundantly proved by the hiftory of European nations, among whom treaties offenfive and defenfive have, with their communication with each other, been conftantly increafing for the two laft centuries; and wars, without becoming lefs frequent, have become far more general, bloody, and expenfive. The balance of power, a notion fpringing up among ftatefmen towards the end of the 15th century, has been a principal caufe both of the frequency and the extenfivenefs of modern wars; the religious diftinctions which divided Europe

after

after the period of the reformation, have also been the caufe or the pretext of frequent hoftilities; and the fuppofed dignity of crowns, an expreffion the more dangerous from the obfcurity of its meaning, has been conftantly enumerated among the reafons which juftified the inhabitants of different countries in rufhing to the deftruction of each other.

Wars thus originating in caufes peculiar to a femi-barbarous ftate of fociety, have been extended in other refpects by the progrefs of knowledge and its effects on the arts. To this we are to attribute many of the improvements in the fcience of deftruction, and in the fcience of finance : to this efpecially we are to attribute the *funding-fyftem*, which at once multiplied the means of warfare twenty-fold, and which, after anticipating and exhaufting the public revenue in almoft every nation of Europe, feems at length to approach the point fo clearly foretold, when it muft produce a fyftem of general peace, or of univerfal defolation.

The Italian Republics, according to Dr. Smith, firft invented funding—from them it paffed to Spain, and from the Spaniards to the reft of the European nations. The practice of funding commenced in England with our national debt during the war which terminated in the peace at Ryfwick in the year 1697, and it has been the means by which this debt has accumulated to its prefent enormous amount. The fyftem itfelf is precifely the fame as to the community, that mortgaging the revenue of an eftate to raife a prefent fum of money, is to the individual. The income mortgaged by the individual arifes perhaps from land, that of the ftate from one or more taxes ; and both in the one cafe and in the other, this mortgage is for the payment of the intereft of the fum borrowed. The individual generally engages to repay the principal when demanded ; the ftate never does this, but while the intereft is regularly difcharged, and the country is tolerably profperous, the fecurity given by the ftate

being

being transferable, finds a ready market, and thus the ab-
forption of the capital, as far as refpects the creditor of the
ftate, is in a great meafure remedied.

The convenience of the funding-fyftem to thofe who adminifter the governments of Europe is obvious.—It enables
them on thè commencement of wars to multiply their refources for the moment, perhaps twenty-fold. Previous to
this invention, a tax raifing five hundred thoufand pounds
annually, would have ftrengthened the hands of government
by this fum only ; but under the funding-fyftem, the tax
being mortgaged for ever for as much money as it will pay
the annual intereft of, brings into the treafury the capital
fum at once, that is, ten or perhaps twelve millions. It is
true this fpendthrift expenditure muft bring a day of reckon-
ing—But what then ? Thofe who adminifter the public revenue are not owners of the eftate, but in general, tenants at
will, or at moft, have a life intereft in it only. The practice of mortgaging the public revenue during wars prevents
the people from feeling the immediate preffure of the expence,
by transferring it in a great meafure to pofterity. Minifters
look to the prefent moment, and delight in expedients that
may delay the evil day.—When it comes, it does not in all
probability fall on thofe with whom the mifchief originated.
They are no longer in power; they are perhaps in their
graves, and removed from the complaints and wrongs of their
injured country.

It is however but candid to acknowledge, that we have
feen you acting on a fuperior fyftem; incurring the odium
of propofing new taxes, to difcharge the intereft of debts con-
tracted in fupport of meafures which you had uniformly oppofed, and teaching almoft an exhaufted people to bear ftill
heavier burthens, rather than facrifice their future good, or
violate the eternal obligations of juftice !—Then was your
day of triumph.

Half

Half informed men have fometimes contended that the national debt is a national good. To enter at large into their arguments is foreign to my purpofe, fince this pofition depends on fophifms that have been often detected. It may indeed be admitted that fome accidental advantages have arifen from the transferable and marketable nature of the fecurities given to the public creditors : In times of commercial profperity thefe have promoted circulation, and acted in fome degree like a quantity of well-fecured paper money : But this effect, befides that it is contingent and uncertain, in no refpect compenfates for the evils arifing from the preffure of taxes, the increafed rate of wages, and the withdrawing of an immenfe capital from productive to unproductive labour *.

Without embarraffing ourfelves with complicated ideas, it may be at once afferted, that a nation which goes on borrowing and mortgaging without redeeming its funds, muft at length, like an individual, become bankrupt, and that the ruin this produces will correfpond to the magnitude of the bankruptcy. This has been all along clearly forefeen by thofe who have examined the fubject ; but the predictions of fome enlightened men, as to the fum of debt under which the nation muft become bankrupt, having turned out fallacious, ignorant perfons have fuppofed that the principle, on which thefe predictions were founded, was in itfelf falfe. But admitting that Mr. Hume † predicted that a debt of a hundred millions would bring on a national bankruptcy, he erred in his calculation only from not forefeeing the influence of the progrefs of knowledge on the ufeful arts, and the increafed fources of re-

* See the Wealth of Nations.

† It does not appear that Mr. Hume was the author of this prediction, which has been generally afcribed to him.—It is however evident from his Effay on Public Credit, that he did not forefee the great amount to which the debt might be carried—a circumftance eafily explained.

venue

venue which would thus be opened. The furprifing advances of chemiftry, and the effects of its application to manufactures ; the wonderful combinations of chemiftry and mechanics, for the reduction of labour—thefe are the happy means by which bankruptcy has been hitherto averted. The fecurity of property and the fpirit of liberty diffufed through the nation, have called forth the talents of our people. Britain has grown profperous in fpite of the wretched politics of her rulers. The genius of Watt, Wedgewood, and Arkwright, has counteracted the expenfe and folly of the American war.

Are we to go on for ever in this extraordinary career * ? It is impoffible ! the fources through which we have been enabled to fuftain our enormous burthens are in a great meafure dried up, our burthens themfelves are increafing, and the whole fabric of our profperity totters to its bafe !

Our profperity depends on commerce ; commerce requires peace, and all the world is at war—this is the fhort and the melancholy hiftory of our fituation. The fhock is felt in England more than elfewhere, becaufe, as was faid before, England is more commercial than any other nation, but it pervades more or lefs the continent of Europe, from St. Peterfburgh to Leghorn : the hiftory of commerce records no calamity fo fevere and fo extenfive. Of the houfes that remain folvent, it is known, that the greater part are ftruggling with difficulties ; that thefe are hourly increafing ; and that diftruft and difmay prevail univerfally. In Britain, as I fhall have occafion to fhew, our mercantile diftreffes are aggravated by the imprudent confidence, arifing out of extra-

---

* I might have anfwered this queftion in the words of Mr. Chalmers, in his " Comparative Eftimate," where he very juftly decides, that we can go on incurring debt, and frefh taxes, only while commerce and manufactures increafe in a correfponding degree. This mafterly work will throw much light on our prefent fituation ; Lord Hawkefbury will do well to perufe it once more.

ordinary

ordinary profperity, which produced a very general over-
trading of capital, and in fome places a fpirit of very unjuftifi-
able fpeculation; but on the continent, where bankruptcy and
diftrefs began firft, the imprudence of the mercantile fyftem
feems to have had little fhare in the failures, which may be
traced almoft entirely to the war politics of the ruling powers,
and the dreadful practices by which thefe have been fupported.

Whoever examines the hiftory of the military eftablifhments of the different European nations, will find that
they have been for more than two hundred years almoft every
where regularly increafing. The means of fupporting this
increafe may have been found, in part, in the gradual aug-
mentation of opulence and population, which perhaps has
taken place pretty generally, in fpite of the burthen of thefe
eftablifhments.—But the very great and fudden increafe of
the armies brought into the field in the latter end of the laft,
and the beginning of the prefent century, is clearly to be attributed to the funding-fyftem, which about this time became
almoft univerfal. From this period the ftanding forces of
Europe during peace have been gradually and regularly aug-
menting as before, and each fucceffive war has produced
more numerous and better appointed armies than that which
preceded.—The forces employed, the expenfe incurred, and
the deftruction produced in the war which terminated in
the peace of 1763, far exceeded whatever was before known
in the annals of hiftory. Satiated and exhaufted with flaughter, the nations of Chriftendom funk down into a fhort-lived
repofe. This was foon difturbed by the emprefs of Ruffia,
whofe reign has involved her fubjects in perpetual diftreffes,
her neighbours in conftant alarms, and has filled the eaftern
parts of Europe with repeated carnage *. In the weft, the
torch

---

* This fingular woman affects to be a patronefs of learning, and is not
deftitute of what are called the princely virtues. She has had a kind of hu-
mour

the torch of war was rekindled by England, an a conflict with her own colonies aided by France, more fruitlefs, fierce, and bloody, than the war of 1756, diffevered her empire, added a hundred millions to her debt, and fix millions annually to her ftanding taxes *.

During thefe operations in the eaft and weft, the centre of Europe was agitated by the reftlefs and pragmatic temper of the Emperor Jofeph. This unwife and unfortunate, but not ill-intentioned prince, was happily controlled by the talents of the great Frederick, who for the laft twenty years of his life cultivated the arts of peace, and on feveral occafions ftifled the flames of a general war. The example of the King of Pruffia, however, and the mutual jealoufy of the continental powers, wonderfully increafed the armies of the continent, and during his reign the peace eftablifhment of Germany, a country containing lefs than eighteen millions of people, rofe to five or fix hundred thoufand foldiers! By his fuperior policy the King of Pruffia indeed contrived to render his army comparatively little burthenfome to his fubjects, and died with his treafury full †. But Auftria and all the inferior powers of Germany have been long very poor. The wants of Jofeph

---

mour of fending her picture in gold fnuff-boxes to literary men in different parts of Europe. Praife has been openly beftowed on her by Zimmermann, and indeed infinuated by Robertfon. Impartial hiftory will record the fteps by which the *wife of Peter III. afcended his throne*; it will tell of 30,000 Turks maffacred in cold blood at Ifmael ; it will defcribe the firft and the fecond divifion of Poland ; and the annalift of better times may record this " auguft patronefs of letters" as the fcourge of the human race.

* By the firft of thefe wars we conquered America, by the fecond we loft it, and thus a balance was ftruck ; but two hundred millions of debt was incurred, and five hundred thoufand lives facrificed !—" What hath pride " profited us ? Or what good have riches with our vaunting brought us ? All " thefe things are paffed away like a fhadow, and as a poft that hafted by."

Wifdom of Solomon.

† His fucceffor, it i. generally underftood, has nearly, if not entirely, diffipated his treafures.

were great, thofe of Leopold greater, and thofe of the prefent Emperor are extreme—Ruffia is abfolutely bankrupt, and the whole body of the peafantry reduced to the moft wretched poverty. Spain languifhes under an immenfe load of debt; and the fame may be faid of Holland, Portugal, and, as I am informed, of the northern powers—The fituation of France needs not to be defcribed.

A philofophical mind will difcover in every page of hiftory, and will lament, while it excufes, the fatal ignorance of thofe by whom nations have been governed. General invectives againft fuch characters are however unjuft; the Rulers of the world ought to be approached with mingled refpect and pity. Supreme power to its proper exercife requires perfect wifdom, and monarchs as well as minifters are weak, fallible and ignorant, like ourfelves. Hence it is that we find them in all ages wafting the little hoards of property acquired by private induftry, in projects of foolifh vanity, or of ftill more foolifh ambition. And hence it is that, during the laft century, we have feen them convert even the acquifitions of fcience and of the arts, rifing unprotected in fociety, to the fame fatal purpofes; carrying the fury of war by this means into the moft remote feas and regions, and exhaufting not only the patrimony of a fingle generation in their rafh and ruinous projects, but that of new generations of men for a long fucceffion of years.

In the order of Providence, great evils bring their own remedies, and the funding-fyftem, by exhaufting the means of fupporting war, has a tendency to produce univerfal peace. But it is melancholy to reflect on the national bankruptcies, which it muft probably render general in the firft inftance. Their effects will vary as the people are more or lefs commercial, more or lefs enlightened. They may for a time rivet the chains of defpotifm, as in Ruffia; or raife a bloody anarchy on the ruins of monarchy, as in France. A fyftem of general peace, adopted fpeedily, may avert a great part of the calamities which hang over Europe; but,

while

while paſſion and prejudice ſo generally predominate, this, alas ! is rather an object of our wiſhes than our hopes.

It ought however to make a deep impreſſion on thoſe who are entruſted with the happineſs of nations, that the direct cauſe of all the troubles in France was the laviſh expenditure of its old government ſupported by the funding-ſyſtem. The war of 1756, and that undertaken for the Americans, brought this ſyſtem to its criſis ; the revenue was more than anticipated by the intereſt of debts and the expenſe of the government ; freſh taxes could not be collected ; the people called loudly for a redreſs of grievances : the court gave way ; popular aſſemblies were ſummoned, and followed each other in rapid ſucceſſion ; the current of opinion ſet ſtronger every day againſt every thing eſtabliſhed : the populace found their ſtrength ; numbers, inſtead of wiſdom, began to govern ; the practice of change begot a habit of changing, and property and principles were ſwept away *.

Happily

* It is the fate of deſpotic governments to be placed in general in the hands of fools ; and where folly commands, it is ignorance alone that can be obedient. Nothing ever was ſo palpably abſurd as the principles on which France mingled in the American war. She wiſhed to weaken England, and threw her force into the American ſcale. We had got into a conteſt which muſt have been long, expenſive, and finally unſucceſsful, even had the abſolute conqueſt of the colonies crowned the firſt years of the war. We were likely, from our pride and prejudices, to perſevere to the uttermoſt, and national bankruptcy could only have arreſted our career. France might have looked on in ſecurity, taken the opportunity of the calm to have arranged her finances, reformed her abuſes, and ſtrengthened herſelf by the arts of peace. She might have riſen on our ruins, the empreſs of the ſea, and the arbitreſs of Europe.—She openly interfered—the diſeaſe which ſeemed lingering and mortal, ſuddenly became violent ; a criſis took place ; we threw off the colonies, acknowledged their independence, and, reaſſuming the arts of peace, became in a few years more proſperous than before. In the mean time France had received a mortal wound ; *to prevent the war from becoming unpopular under the exiſting burthens,* ſhe had carried it on without new taxes,

by

Happily for England, by great and virtuous exertions, she escaped in the year 1783 the bankruptcy which France incurred. The effects of continued peace on a nation such as ours are beyond calculation. National confidence and credit being restored, our manufactures spread over the continents of the old and the new world, and our revenue rose on *the basis of circulation* to its late unexampled height. A paper currency of promissory notes and of bills of exchange was a necessary consequence, and this, which ought to have represented specie or merchandise only, became in a season of singular prosperity the representation of almost every kind of property fixed and unfixed.

In the mean time affairs on the continent assumed a hostile aspect. The allied powers began to arm; France

by borrowing only. When peace came, this new debt was to be provided for—the people were poor, discontented, and, what was worst of all, they were in some degree enlightened—the rest is known.

The policy of the powers which are combined against France is of the same weak and foolish kind. The folly and the crimes of France rendered a civil war inevitable, and Europe might have looked on in safety and peace. This mighty people, weakened by intestine divisions, would have been no longer formidable; and the process of their experiments on government, if left to itself, would have been fruitful of lessons of the most important kind. The neighbouring monarchs met at Pillnitz, and agreed to invade France the first *convenient opportunity.* The treaty was discovered; it gave victory to the republicans without a contest; a civil war was prevented; and the banner of Jacobinism reigned triumphant. The allied powers have carried their treaty into effect; but being burthened with debt already, and the state of the public mind *requiring to be particularly consulted at present,* they are, like France of old, carrying it on by borrowing without laying on taxes, leaving this for the season of peace. The Emperor I am told gives nine per cent. for money, to prevent the imposition of taxes; and yet it is said that the unreasonable people of Vienna are not satisfied.

So far the policy of the powers now allied against France, and that of France herself in the American war, are precisely similar—How far the effects may correspond is in the womb of time.

armed

armed alfo. Armaments, in countries comparatively fpeaking little commercial, required fpecie. It probably flowed freely from England, for a paper circulation fupplied its place. Thefe armaments rendered the people, as well as the governments, poor, by diminifhing and opprefling productive labour, abforbing the wealth that fhould have been employed in private induftry, and obftructing commercial intercourfe. Hence our cuftomers did not purchafe, or did not pay for our manufactures, and they began to remain on our hands.

Certain circumftances however prevented for a time our feeling the full effect of the war politics on the continent. In the firft place we were at peace, and had declared for a peace-fyftem, while the reft of Europe was agitated, and under arms. Hence our funds became a favourite object of purchafe for thofe monied men on the continent who wifhed to fecure their property; immenfe fums, it is faid, flowed in from France and the Low Countries, and the prices of ftock rofe for a time, with the decline of our export of manufactures, and the efflux, as it fhould feem, of the precious metals.

Another circumftance operated in our favour. The war on the continent increafed the demand for particular manufactures, from Germany, and more efpecially from France—Birmingham felt this, fo did Yorkfhire. Burning for combat, the *Sans Culottes* rufhed into the field—and Arms! Arms and clothing! was echoed from Picardy to Provence. Thefe demands could only be fupplied by England. France had ruined her credit by her fecond revolution: fhe muft come to market with fpecie; and her gold and filver might have refted with us.—Our true policy was clear.

By this time however the fympathies of the different parties in England were excited to fuch a degree by the ftate of things on the continent, that the dictates of found reafon
could

could no longer be heard; and the wickednefs of the ruling party in France having perpetrated one deliberate and dreadful murder, calculated to awake the horror of men in an extraordinary degree, the original friends of the revolution became mute; the once facred name of Liberty itfelf became offenfive; the alarmifts rofe fuddenly in numbers and force; clamours and indignation fprung up in every quarter; and, amidft a wild uproar of falfe terrors and of virtuous fympathy, the nation was plunged headlong into this dreadful war!

One powerful voice indeed was heard above the ftorm, but the accents of reafon and truth founded like treafon to an irritated people, and our rulers joined in the general outcry; the friends of peace incurred the fouleft calumnies of the day, but fecured to themfelves the pureft admiration, when paffion and prejudice fhall be no more.

War came; and faft on its heels a dreadful train of evils—bankruptcy followed bankruptcy in rapid fucceffion, our refources feemed to vanifh, diftruft and terror feifed the mercantile world, and the Bank of England itfelf partook, as it is reported, of the general alarm. In the mean time you are faid to have declared in your place, that thefe evils had no connexion with the war, and Mr. Dundas affured us that they arofe from our extraordinary profperity. Similar language is made ufe of by the partizans of adminiftration every where, and it is fit that this dreadful error fhould be publicly unveiled.

In a feafon of general peace and great profperity, private as well as public credit had arifen to an extraordinary height, and, from caufes very obvious, but which it would be tedious to enumerate, paper-money became in a great meafure the medium of circulation. This paper confifted of two kinds; of bills of exchange payable at different dates, and generally difcountable; and of promiffory notes, iffued by the Bank of England and private Banking-houfes, payable in

fpecie

fpecie on demand. The credit of each of thefe depended on their reprefenting a property real and fecure. The promiffory notes were indeed fuppofed to reprefent fpecie at all times ready on demand, but in reality refted for their credit on the bafis of fome fixed property within the kingdom, and frequently on landed eftates. The bills of exchange depended for their circulation on the joint credit of the drawer and the acceptor, and reprefented in a great meafure property out of the kingdom ; perhaps on the feas, in the Weft Indies, on the coaft of Africa, in America, or on the continent of Europe *. By means of this medium a vaft quantity of fixed property was brought, as it were, into a ftate of activity ; the paper money in circulation, every kind included, amounting, as I have been told, to a fum that feems almoft incredible † ! The effects of a war on a paper medium, fuch as I have defcribed, may be eafily imagined.—It muft diminifh the fecurity of all property on the feas, in our iflands, on the coaft of Africa, &c. and of courfe deftroy or impair the credit of all bills of exchange running on the validity of fuch property. If the property itfelf during a war would not eafily find a purchafer, neither would a bill refting on that property. The property itfelf however might ftill be fale able, though at a diminifhed value ; but this would not be the cafe with a bill of exchange, which, if it does not pafs for the fum it is drawn for, will pafs for nothing, and is thrown out of circulation. The manner in which this diftreffed our Weft-India houfes is well known. The degree of hazard of our iflands was perhaps over-rated, a circumftance arifing from the peculiar nature of the war,

---

* This fubject is very elegantly and fully explained in a pamphlet intitled " Thoughts on the Caufe of the prefent Failures," publifhed by Johnfon.

† Two hundred millions.

and the fears under which we laboured, and still labour, of the desperate methods to which the French may have recourse. Previous to the war in England, bankruptcies had begun on the continent, and the security of bills of foreign exchange was every day impaired. The invasion of Holland by Dumourier, one of the first consequences of the war, was a blow aimed at the credit of all Europe ; our houses concerned in Dutch and other foreign exchanges found their security particularly shaken ; many of them are supposed to have tottered, and several fell. A similar effect took place in various parts of the continent, and the action and reaction of ruin spread far and wide. The invasion and partition of Poland contributed much to this general calamity. The Bank of Warsaw, the deposit of all the surplus wealth of the landed interest of Poland, was oppressed and destroyed by the royal plunderers ; it failed, as it is said, for ten millions sterling, and brought down with it various houses throughout Europe, particularly in Petersburg, Hamburg, and Amsterdam *.

The war deprived our manufactures of the French market, of all others the most extensive, and, as it had been conducted for a twelvemonth past, by far the most safe and lucrative. The general wreck of credit among our allies on the continent deprived us in a great measure of the markets there. Orders did not arrive, or, if they did arrive, could not be executed ; the security of the correspondent was doubted, or the channel of payment shut up. It was soon therefore found, that our manufactures for the foreign markets had not sustained a temporary check, such as arises from overtrading every sixth or seventh year of peace, but an absolute stagnation ; the bills and paper running on the security of the capital vested in machinery (an enormous and lately most

---

* Fifteen houses in Petersburg, concerned in the trade to China, failed together.

productive

productive property) were of courfe fhaken in their credit, and in the courfe of a few weeks, if a profpect of peace does not open, will be of all others the moft infecure. If it were proper on fuch an occafion to bring forward names, each of thefe affertions might be fupported and illuftrated by abundant proofs.

The general refult of thefe particulars is—That whereas, before the war, bills were difcountable, and of courfe entered into circulation from every part of the world, at perhaps eighteen months date, and fometimes at even longer, diftruft and bankruptcy have, for the prefent, rendered three-fourths of the whole wafte paper; and thofe of the very firft credit are in general negotiable at two months date only. The immenfe chafm that this muft make in circulation may be eafily imagined.

This general diftrefs in the commercial and manufacturing interefts muft, of courfe, occafion a great preffure on the monied men. What is their fituation? Their property is generally vefted in public fecurities; thefe muft be fold out to meet the exigence, at a lofs of from 20 to 25 per cent. Public fecurities have already funk in value in confequence of the war, to the amount of nearly fifty millions fterling, a fum almoft equal to the whole of our national debt at the commencement of the war of 1755!

Land has not efcaped deterioration; but, for obvious reafons, except in the immediate vicinity of towns, it has fuffered lefs than any other property; and of courfe the fecurity of promiffory notes iffued by country banking-houfes, as far as they depended on landed eftates, is, or ought to be, lefs affected than any other. In the general panic, indeed, runs have been made on almoft every houfe of this kind; a few have failed from infufficient ftability, and many have ftopped payment for want of fpecie. But in general thofe who have

fhewn

shewn a sufficient foundation of real property, have been supported by public confidence, and, in the absolute scarcity of gold and silver, their notes have returned into circulation. In situations where this has happened, the distress is far less than where no circulation of such promissory notes had taken place. It seems the more necessary to state these facts, because, in both houses of parliament, some respectable individuals seem disposed to impute our present distresses in a great measure to the increase of banking-houses issuing promissory notes *.

It may be observed, that circulating notes of this kind, each representing a guinea, have long been the universal medium throughout Scotland, where the commercial distress, though great, is much less than in England; not more than one banking-house there having as yet failed. Five pound notes of the same kind are in common circulation through several of the northern counties, and, in the moment of general panic, were much exclaimed against. But the alarm is subsiding, and confidence returns †. The truth will soon appear to be, that a well-secured and well-regulated—medium of this kind is at this instant of essential service where it circulates; and it is very probable that it will be resorted to in situations where it has not yet been adopted. In Lancashire, where the distress both in the commercial and manufacturing interests is perhaps greater than in any part of the kingdom, promissory notes were never issued by any of the banking-houses; and to this, I will venture to say, the universal stagnation there is in some degree to be attributed. The necessity of resorting to a paper-money generally, which cannot be immediately commuted into specie, would indeed be a

* The Duke of Norfolk is one who has fallen into this mistake.

† See the proceedings at Newcastle, Whitehaven, &c.

proof

proof of extraordinary diftrefs, but it may one day come.
There is a fituation that a good citizen muft brood over in
filence, but which the rapid career of our adverfity does not
admit to be long abfent from his thoughts, in which it may
be the only national remedy againft general ruin and confufion.

Though the banking-houfes which circulate promiffory
notes have not contributed in any confiderable degree to
our prefent diftrefs, it muft be admitted that it has been
aggravated by the imprudence of individuals in over-trading
their capitals, and reforting in feveral inftances to the fyftem
of drawing and redrawing for fupporting their credit*. This
however is a difeafe which has a conftant tendency to
arife in feafons of great profperity, and which, though it
operate feverely on particular places, cannot be confidered as
entering largely into our national diftrefs:—not having been
without its effect, it gives I prefume a colour to the affertion
of Mr. Dundas; but will even Mr. Dundas fay, that the
imprudence of a few individuals has deftroyed the whole
market of our manufactures, or lowered the funds fifty millions?

To this general reprefentation an objection will perhaps
occur, that it explains things too clearly; that events can
feldom be traced in this regular way; and that politics do
not afford any thing fo nearly approaching to demonftration.
The reply to this is eafy—Politics have generally for their
object the conduct of cabinets; and the uncertainty to
which they are liable is chiefly to be imputed to the ignorance and caprice by which cabinets are governed. Hence
the difficulty of predicting how they may act arifes from

---

* Thofe who wifh to fee this clearly and fully explained, may con-
fult the Wealth of Nations, laft edition.

the

the impoffibility of forefeeing, with any certainty, their motives of action. But that part of the political œconomy
which unfolds the theory of trade and manufactures, ap-
proaches to the nature of fcience, becaufe it has the intercourfe of commercial men for its object, who are conftantly
governed by a fenfe of intereft, the moft uniform motive of
human conduct. We diftinguifh ill, if we fuppofe that what
refpects commerce is equally uncertain with what refpects
politics; the freaks of the mifchievous monkey are indeed
wild and capricious, but the actions of the induftrious beaver
are uniform and exact. It may alfo be objected to this
explanation of the caufes of our diftrefs, that it is founded
on principles which apply to former wars as well as to that
we are engaged in, while our prefent calamities are altogether
fingular and unprecedented. It muft be admitted that our
diftreffes are fingular in degree, but they are not fingular in
their nature; in the commencement of all our wars, induftry
and credit have fuftained a fimilar blow, and it only remains
to be fhewn why the prefent fhock is fo peculiarly fevere and
tremendous.

That the entrance of war has always injured our commercial profperity, may be proved from the authentic documents in Mr. Chalmers's " Comparative Eftimate;" and
thofe who remember the commencement of the laft war,
muft alfo recollect the diftrefs which it occafioned. The
extraordinary ruin of the prefent moment, compared with
that of 1755 or 1775, is to be traced to the change which
this nation, as well as the other nations of Europe, has been
gradually undergoing, and to the peculiar nature and feat of
the exifting warfare. At the breaking out of the war in
1755, the debt of Great Britain amounted to feventy-two
millions; and now the debt funded and unfunded is nearly
two hundred and fifty millions. We fet out on the prefent
occafion

occafion under an additional weight of almoft two hundred millions!

But let us take the commencement of the laft war, a period ftill frefh in our recollections, and when the difparity of fituation was not fo great. In the beginning of February, you held out a profpect that the exifting revenue was not likely to fall off in confequence of the prefent hoftilities, becaufe in the firft year of the laft war it was not much affected. You feemed to admit that the *progrefs* of our commerce and manufactures might indeed be ftopped, but you did not apprehend there would be much, if any, diminution of what we already poffeffed. The melancholy records of the laft three months have detected this fatal error, to which perhaps the war itfelf is in fome degree owing, and, painful as is the office, there may yet be fome advantage in tracing it to its fource. The American war commenced in a gradual manner—Our difputes with the colonifts had been of feveral years continuance, and before hoftilities broke out our merchants had forefeen them and provided againft them. The provifion, it is true, was far from complete ; for though in the year immediately preceding the war very unufual remittances were made from America, yet, on the opening of hoftilities, a large capital was locked up in that country, by which the trade of London, Briftol, and Liverpool, was confiderably injured, and at Glafgow and Whitehaven a very extenfive bankruptcy took place. A circumftance however diftinguifhed thofe times from the prefent, which is of material importance.—Previous to the war of 1775, our manufacturers were not much in the habit of exporting on their own accounts. They received their orders chiefly from the merchants here, at whofe rifque the manufactures were fhipped ; fo that though the mercantile houfes received a fevere blow in the rupture with America, the manufacturing

capital

capital was, comparatively fpeaking, little injured. What contributed a good deal to this, was the prohibition of importation laid by the American Congrefs the year before the war, at a time when remittances to this country were allowed, and were fo confiderable. In confequence of this, our manufacturers, with their fkill and their capitals unimpaired, began early to explore new markets, and to improve thofe already known; and from this date commenced that rapid increafe of export to the continent of Europe, which faved us from national bankruptcy, and raifed us again to our rank among nations. It was foon found that the American market was, comparatively fpeaking, of little value; and it was found alfo, that the fuperiority of our manufactures forced their way into it, notwithftanding the obftructions of the war. They took a circuitous courfe indeed through Holland; but Yorkfhire furnifhed the greater part of the clothing of the Sans Culottes of America; and though they had fet up a republican government, and were rebels, not againft Louis XVI. but our own gracious King—no Traitorous Correfpondence Bill was moved for by the Attorney General of the day*.

Since the laft peace however our manufacturers have almoft univerfally acted as merchants, and fhipped their goods on their own account. They have gained poffeffion of

---

* It was during this period, if my memory does not fail me, that the Duke of Richmond, who has been fo loyally employed of late in fortifying the Tower, was accufed in the minifterial papers of having furveyed fome parts of the coaft, for the purpofe of directing the French where they might with fafety attack us; it was at this time that Mr. Burke openly boafted in the Houfe of Commons, of correfponding with the republican-rebel Franklin, intriguing at Paris to bring all Europe on our heads; it was during the fame calamitous period that a young Statefman, fince fo well known throughout Europe, began his career, by juftifying the republicans of America in their refiftance, and reprobating, as the height of wickednefs and infanity, our defign of fubjugating them by force.

the

the foreign markets, in part from the fuperiority of their
fkill, but far more from the fuperiority of their capital,
which has enabled them to give a credit almoft every where
from twelve to eighteen months. Hence at the prefent moment our manufacturing capital (contrary to what happened
in the beginning of the laft war) is in a great meafure invefted in foreign debts. The merchants in the ports of the
kingdom felt the calamities of war fooneft; but it is on the
manufacturing body that it will fall with the moft unrelenting ruin. What adds to the diftrefs of the moment is, that
the war was not, like the American conteft, long forefeen.
We had declared for a peace-fyftem; it was clearly our intereft to maintain it; it feemed almoft fuicide in France to
provoke a quarrel: mercantile men in both kingdoms deprecated a rupture, and, reafoning on the grounds of mutual
intereft (the familiar and fundamental principle of plain
and fenfible men), they could not believe, long after the
horizon began to darken, that a ftorm would enfue—
When the clouds burft, they were therefore naked and un-
prepared.

The difference in the fituation of our public burthens is
alfo to be confidered in comparing the two periods; we commenced the war with America under a debt of 130 millions;
and we ftart now with a debt of 250:—our peace eftablifhment, the intereft of the debt included, was then ten millions annually; it has now mounted to feventeen millions.

It may however be fuppofed that our ability to pay thefe
increafed burthens has increafed in a proportional degree—
I would not undervalue the refources of my country, and I
believe this to be true; but it is only true while we continue
at peace, and preferve as much as poffible the peace of the
world. If indeed our ability to pay taxes were meafured by
the ftate of our exports, it might be juftly doubted whether

7   it

it has augmented in the degree that is fuppofed *. But this
ability depends in reality on the excefs of our productive
labour over our wants; and the facility of collecting taxes, a
point very important, depends in a great meafure on the degree of confumption and circulation.—The excefs of our productive labour does not appear in our exports, as fome are
apt to fuppofe, for much of it has been employed in the
creation of new capital—in the increafe of buildings and machinery—in the improvement of the foil—and in the opening
of new roads and canals, of all modes of employing the national capital by far the moft ufeful †. Thefe improvements
were going on with a moft happy and accelerated progrefs;
our public burthens were beginning to decreafe with the increafe of our power of bearing them; and England advanced
rapidly towards that ultimate point of profperity, the poffi-
bility of which was demonftrated by Dr. A. Smith with a
mathematical precifion; and its approach predicted by yourfelf in a ftrain of eloquence that gave to truth all the charms

---

* The average of our exports for the laft ten years does not, it is faid,
exceed feventeen millions; which is not more than three millions greater
than the amount they averaged in an equal number of years before the American war. The documents on this fubject however are not fufficient for
accurate ftatement.

See *Mr. Chalmers's Comparative Eftimate.*

† In Lancafhire alone, one million of the profits of manufactures and
commerce is about to be invefted in canals now forming there, if the diftreffes of the times permit the fubfcriptions to be paid; and fuch of the labouring manufacturers as are employed at all, are now chiefly employed in
forming thefe canals. The happy effects of fuch an application of capital in
a fingle county, and fuch a county as Lancafhire, no one can eftimate, but
they depend almoft entirely on peace. The war has already funk the value
of fhares in this property greatly, and it has diminifhed the carriage on the
canals already made, more than one half. On this fubject authentic infor-
mation may be obtained from the Duke of Bridgewater. I fpeak on the
authority of a well-informed correfpondent.

of

of fiction, and unfolded to an admiring nation, a prospect of real happiness, supposed only to exist in the poet's dream * ! You knew, however, and you acknowledged, that the continuation of peace was necessary to ensure the blessings you foretold—happy had it been for the nation, if you had seen that it was indispensable to the duration of those we already enjoyed !

It has been imagined by many, that the present war ought to be light in comparison of the last, because then we fought alone, and now all the world is in alliance with us. Mr. Dundas in the House of Commons boasted of this; and declared the intention of ministry was to bring, if possible, every nation of Europe upon France. It is, I presume, in consequence of the operations of this policy, before it was avowed, that Spain and Prussia are now in arms, and that Portugal, Turkey, and the Northern Powers, are openly solicited to join the general confederacy—Weak and miserable policy ! Better far had it been for Britain to have fought France singly, if her power had been twice as great, while the rest of Europe looked on, than to stir up and mingle in this general crusade of folly and ruin. I speak not in the language of a moralist, but of a politician ; and of this assertion I challenge the most rigid examination.—What supported us during the American war ? the export of our manufactures to countries that could purchase them, because they enjoyed the blessings of peace. But who is there now to buy our manufactures ? where is peace now to be found ? The nations of Europe are in arms from the White Sea to the Pillars of Hercules, and in the course of the summer there will be upwards of two millions of men in the field. Ancient or modern history states

* See Mr. Pitt's speech, 17th Feb. 1792, on his motion for taking off a part of our taxes.

E

nothing

nothing equal to the expenfe or the extent of this armament, undertaken when the funds of all the belligerent powers are anticipated and exhaufted, and national credit is everywhere (England I hope excepted) about to explode. If the whole population of Europe be a hundred and twenty millions, it will contain twenty-five or thirty millions of men fit for labour, or what are called fighting men. Of this number there is a 12th or 15th part taken from a productive labour to that which produces nothing; or, what illuftrates the point more clearly, brought into the fame fituation with refpect to the public as if the whole became paralytic in a day, and yet required not only the fame fubfiftence as when capable of labour, but one much more expenfive. But as the men called into the field are in the flower of life, the productive labour diminifhed will be more than in proportion to their numbers; and as they are to combat far from home, the expenfe of their maintenance while foldiers will double and treble what mere ceffation from labour would have produced. The ftock of productive labour muft however not only be fubject to all former burthens, but oppreffed with the maintenance of the labourers taken from it and turned into foldiers, and thus the lofs will be more than doubled. It is poffible that in fome parts of Europe famine may arife, but this is not likely to be a general or an immediate effect. Subfiftence is fuch an evident want, and fuch an irreftible call, that the ground will always be cultivated in the firft inftance. The labourers taken from agriculture for the field, will have their places fupplied by others deprived of their ufual labour in manufactures, which the war has injured or ruined; and poverty, by teaching men lefs expenfive habits both of diet and clothing, will protract the hour of abfolute want. It is in the feat of war only that famine may be confidered as inevitable; it is there alfo that difeafe may foon be expected; contagion will fcatter her poifon, and deftroy more than the fword. The

elafticity

elafticity of human exertions cannot be exactly calculated; and it would be rafh to predict, how, or to what extent thefe may operate under burthens fo heavy and fo general. It feems however unavoidable that, during the continuance of the war, thefe burthens muft every where increafe. If the fupport of life becomes even difficult, the collection of reve- nue will become impoffible: from the fhrivelled mufcles and dried bones of their ftarving peafantry, the conquerors of Poland and the invaders of France will not be able to extract the fupport of their fenfelefs ambition and foolifh wafte.

It is evident that this general poverty muft operate pe- culiarly, and every day more heavily, on Britain. Since the laft war this country has become the ftore-houfe of the na- tions of Europe, and has furnifhed almoft the whole ftock of the fuperfluities they have been enabled to buy. We fee clearly that it is the confumption of thefe fuperfluities which the war muft firft deftroy; experience has rendered this truth inconteftible. Thofe who live by the manufacture of thefe fuperfluities, muft therefore be the firft and greateft fufferers in every part of Europe, and unfortunately the greater part of this defcription of men live here. Here then the ruin muft be moft feverely felt, and our fufferings will be the greater and the harder to bear, becaufe they will be in the exact proportion of our former *profperity*. It is very clear then, that had we even ourfelves continued at peace, while the other belligerent powers were at war, we fhould have fuffered much from the progrefs of univerfal poverty.— There are however advantages attending fuch a fituation, which, with prudent management, might have born us through the difficulties. We fhould have fupplied the clothing of the various armies in the field; we fhould have enjoyed a monopoly of the fale of arms, artillery, and the other means of deftruction; we fhould have become the uni- verfal carriers of provifions and warlike ftores; we fhould

E 2

have

have been enabled to convey our own manufactures in safety wherever any sale for them remained ; and we should have been saved the enormous and destructive expense of arming and protecting our extended commerce in the different quarters of the globe. Our possessions in the east and in the west would have remained secure, and the credit of our paper circulation continued unimpaired. While the storm raged on the land, England might have declared the ocean inviolable ; and if the warring powers had disturbed it, she might have reared her head above the waves, extended her immortal trident, and bid the tempest be still *. Holding in her possession a great part of the clothing, the arms, and the stores of the powers at war, and being at the same time the undisputed mistress of the sea, and the great channel of intercourse between nations—when the strength and fury of conflicting passions were sated with blood, or subdued with slaughter, she might have denounced her vengeance on the aggressors, have offered her succours to the oppressed, and dictated the term of univerfal peace.—Such our situation might have been—nay, must have been, had we not become parties in the general strife. What is our situation now ? We are involved ourselves in the quarrel ; there is no nation of Europe left to mediate between the conflicting powers ; and if England does not again assume the office of umpire, nothing but the extermination of the French , or the downfall of the governments of Germany, seems capable of satisfying the enraged parties, or restoring the peace of the world. But it may be said, it is better for us to fight France now with all the world with us, than to fight her hereafter alone. Why should we fight her at all ?—it is not our interest.   But it

---

* Maturate fugam, regique hæc dicite vestro:
Non illi imperium pelagi, faevumque tridentem ;
Sed mihi forte datum.——— VIRGIL. Æn. I.

may be fuppofed that the ambition of France, when her government is fettled, will compel us to go to war in felf-de-
fence. I do not think this likely, becaufe it cannot be *her*
intereft; but we will allow the fuppofition. If France attack
us, it muft be on the fea, our favourite element, and there
fhe will, I doubt not, find our fuperiority once more.—There
fhe found our fuperiority in the American conteft, though fhe
employed her whole refources on her marine, though fhe
was aided by Spain, Holland and America, and though fhe
attacked us when we were in fome degree exhaufted by three
expenfive and bloody campaigns.

If France and England combat alone, it muft be on the
fea, and deftructive though the conteft muft be, it is not
likely of itfelf either to endanger our conftitution or deftroy
our credit, as fome have weakly fuppofed. Our conftitution
is enthroned in the hearts of Englifhmen, and will never be
deftroyed by foreign force; our credit depends on our commerce, but more efpecially on our manufactures, which we
know by experience can furvive a rupture with France, and
even increafe during its continuance, *provided the reft of
Europe is at peace* *. Unfortunately at prefent all Europe is
not only engaged in war, but in a war of unexampled defpe-
ration and expenfe, at a time when public debts and taxes
have accumulated to an enormous degree in almoft every
one of the belligerent powers; where the governments (that
of our own country always excepted) are univerfally oppreffive, and the people poor and wretched.

* I would not however be underftood to confider a war with France, or
with any other country, in any other light under our circumftance, than in
that of a moft ferious calamity. I wifh to point out the peculiarity in the prefent war, that makes it to us particularly deftructive. It is the general ftate of
warfare, and the confequent poverty, that is our bane. In regard to fome of
the powers now under arms, if they are to be at war, it is of little confequence
to us, as to the actual force they can bring forward, whether they fight with
or againft us.

Fifty

Fifty years ago, Mr. Hume, treating on the effects of public credit, obferved, that it muft either deftroy the nation, or the nation muft deftroy it. " I muft confefs," fays this profound obferver, " when I fee princes and ftates " quarrelling, amidft their debts, funds, and public mort- " gages, it always brings to my mind a match of cudgel- " playing fought in a china fhop *." Since the time this was written, the public debts of the European nations have been more than doubled, taking the whole together, and thofe of France, Britain, and Ruffia, have increafed almoft fourfold. The figure of Mr. Hume may now perhaps be a little altered. The prefent match of cudgel-playing is indeed in a china-fhop, but the walls of the houfe are now become china alfo. If the performers get very warm in the bufinefs, they may therefore not only deftroy the moveables, but bring the houfe itfelf about their ears.

I heard a member in the Houfe of Commons pleading with great eloquence for our plunging into the war with France, and call out—Perifh our commerce, if it muft perifh, but let our conftitution live !—The words were foolifh :— the feparation is no longer poffible. The vital principle of our conftitution—the divifion and diftribution of its powers, may indeed furvive the ruin of commerce; and provided the whole people be enlightened, it may be perpetuated after the wreck of our power. The fpirit of our religion may be preferved after the decay of our riches, and poverty and forrow may even render it more pure. The equal principle of our laws, now contained and exemplified in five hundred volumes in folio, may appear perhaps as beautiful, when the deftruction of property fhall have rendered 499 volumes of ftatutes obfolete, and a fingle volume comprifes all that our poverty demands. But the bleffings of our conftitution, in the eye of thofe who adminifter, or hope to adminifter its

* Effay on Public Credit.

powers,

powers, depend, I conceive, on our opulence, and muſt periſh with the commerce from which that opulence flows. Let thoſe therefore who wiſh for *things as they are*, beware of war: true patriots, who abhor civil convulſions, will cheriſh the arts of peace.

"Periſh our commerce"—fooliſh words! What affords three millions annually to the poor? A million and a half annually to the church? What ſupplies a million to the civil liſt?—Our commerce. What ſupports the expenſe of our immenſe naval and military eſtabliſhments? All our places and penſions?—What but our commerce? Thirteen millions of our taxes depend on circulation and conſumption, and this thoughtleſs ſenator cries out—"Periſh our commerce, let our conſtitution live!" But how then muſt the neceſſary ſplendour, the patronage, and the far more extenſive influence of the crown be ſupported? And if this ſplendour, patronage, and influence are ſwept away—where is our conſtitution? What ſhall maintain the crown againſt a band of factious nobles cajoling the people with the ſound of liberty to cover their ſelfiſh ambition; or what ſhall defend hereditary honours and property of every kind againſt the great maſs of the nation, now become poor, and therefore deſperate; ravenous, perhaps, from their wants, and terrible from the remainder of ſpirit and pride which has deſcended from better times * ?

Our conſtitution and our commerce have grown up together; their connection was not at firſt a neceſſary one perhaps, but events have rendered it ſuch; the peace and the ſafety of England depend on its being preſerved. Our very habits and manners, and the ſtructure of ſociety among us, are founded on this union. I know the evils of our ſituation, but the heavy load of our debts and taxes muſt teach us to ſubmit. Patience, peace, œconomy, and gradual re-

* The author can throw out hints only at preſent; but in favour of the prerogative of the crown, as things are ſituated, be has much to offer.

formation,

formation, are the remedies that wife men would point out; the chance of more dangerous means being reforted to arifes from the folly of one clafs, who deny thefe evils, and by denying aggravate them; and from the folly of another, who pronounce them intolerable, and would liften to the counfels of enthufiafts or knaves. At prefent, never was a nation more fubmiffive, or more loyal; but a wife minifter will not wantonly try our patience or goad us too much.

"Perifh our commerce!"—Let the member for Norwich correct his expreffion. We will excufe the inaccuracy of an ardent and eloquent mind; we will even make allowance for the prejudices of education—In the fchool of Mr. Burke, trade and manufactures are words that found meanly: among the Jefuits of St. Omer's, the words themfelves were perhaps unknown. Early education, natural tafte, and peculiar fublimity of imagination, have made, I prefume, the detail and the exactnefs of commerce difgufting to Mr. Burke; and have furnifhed his mind with thofe grand and obfcure ideas, that affociate with the lofty manners of chivalry, and the Gothic gloom of a darker age. Hence, probably (fince time, by extinguifhing ambition, has reftored the original habits of his mind), we are to explain his ftrong preference of the feudal relicks of our conftitution, and his dread of the progrefs of commerce, as leading to innovation and change. I do not wifh to break a lance with the champion of ariftocracy, or with any of his followers; and I would concede in their favour as much as truth will admit. If our fociety were to be caft anew, if the interefts of our country were alone to be confulted, and the means were entirely at our command—much as commerce is to be valued, it would be wifer and better to give it lefs fhare in our profperity, and at all events to render our revenue independent of foreign trade. How far it might be defirable to control its effects on our manners, and on our habits of

thinking,

thinking, is a queſtion that I cannot enter on at preſent. Conſulting our taſte, and ſetting moral conſiderations aſide, we ſhould perhaps be willing to preſerve a greater degree of correctneſs and purity of manners, and more of the nice and high-ſpirited ſenſe of honour, than commerce generally admits. But if we try different characters by the teſt of utility, and found this teſt on the actual ſtate of the nation, the knight of chivalry and his various offspring, compared to the modern manufacturer or the merchant, ſeem weak and uſeleſs things. Even the country gentleman of England, the moſt reſpectable character of all thoſe *lilies of the valley who neither toil nor ſpin*, ſinks in this compariſon. The proprietor of landed property, who lives on the income of his eſtates, can in general be conſidered only as the conduit that conveys the wealth of one generation to another. He is a neceſſary link in ſociety indeed, but his place can at all times be eaſily ſupplied: in this point of view the poor peaſant who cultivates his eſtate is of more importance than he. How then ſhall we eſtimate him when compared with a reſpectable manufacturer—with the original genius, for inſtance, who has found means to convert our clay into porcelain, and lays all Europe under contribution to England by his genius, taſte, and ſkill? Or what rank will he take, when his exertions are put in competition with the power and enterpriſe of the merchant, whoſe ſhips viſit the moſt remote ſhores and nations; to whom the coaſts of Aſia and America are familiar; who draws his wealth from the wilds of Nootka or Labrador, and who makes the diſtant Pacific yield up its ſtores? Even in his more elevated ſituation in the houſe of commons, the country gentleman, however eloquent and virtuous (Mr. Wyndham himſelf), muſt not be compared, as an object of national conſequence, with a character like this.

To the conſiderations which I have offered on the im-

F   portance

portance of commerce and manufactures, and on the effects already produced on them by the war, you, Sir, if you were more in the habit of explaining ministerial conduct, might perhaps reply—That the war is a war of necessity—that it is likely to be short and successful—and that, at all events, the dignity of the nation (the phrase used in the American war), or perhaps of the crown (for this is now the more correct expression of Lord Grenville), is concerned in carrying it on. On each of these points I mean to offer a few observations. I will then endeavour to shew the state the nation is likely to be in, on the recess of parliament; I will make some observations on the terrible responsibility that ministers assume, and conclude with one or two remarks addressed more particularly to yourself.

The war was necessary, as its supporters say; and this necessity is explained in different ways.—By a few it is asserted, that the French were determined to quarrel with us, and that they declared war against us at a time when it was unexpected and unprovoked. This language however is held by very few, and is indeed so utterly inconsistent both with fact and probability, that nothing but ignorance or disingenuousness can employ it. The French were fighting, or thought they were fighting, for their national existence, against a combination of the most alarming kind—To what purpose should they add England to the number of their enemies?—England, whose power they knew by fatal experience—whose irresistible force on the ocean they had repeatedly sunk under—and whose neutrality seemed almost essential to their procuring the means of carrying on the war. If it be asserted that they hoped to excite commotions among us, peace seemed necessary to this scheme; for during peace only could they carry on the intercourse which such a plan would require. Idle threats of internal commotions were indeed thrown out by some individuals among them; but that these

commotions

commotions would be directly promoted by an open war, this, could only be sincerely expected by men who were before insane. It may however be said, that insanity did in reality pervade their councils, or those at least by whom their councils were influenced; and indeed this supposition seems in a great measure founded on truth. But the reply to this is clear: how far soever their insanity might go, it did not extend to a war with England, a calamity not only deprecated by their rulers, but by the whole body of the people. There is not an individual who has been in France since the revolution, who will not confirm this truth*. The manner in which this fierce nation humbled itself to England in negociation, was indeed very remarkable; and though in a moment of wounded pride, the actual declaration of war came from them, yet they soon repented of their conduct, and are now openly renewing their endeavours, one might almost say, their solicitations, for peace†. Peace and war, Mr. Pitt, were in your choice—they are in your choice now; you made your election of the latter—you adhere to it—to the late application of Le Brun, it is said, you have not even vouchsafed an answer.

It might seem, indeed, from the whole of your conduct towards France for a twelvemonth past, that England had a particular interest in the continuance of war; or, if she is supposed to be too proud to be governed by her sense of interest, that her honour was concerned in the keeping up of

* The National Assembly had probably been deceived respecting the sentiments of the people of this country, but previous to the war they had discovered their error. The decree of the 19th November might perhaps be somewhat influenced by their notion of the existence of a republican spirit here, and in this respect the addresses from different bodies of Englishmen did great mischief. But the effects of the proclamation had shewn the real temper of the nation in a clear and striking light, and this was well understood in France when they were negociating for peace.

† See the Letters of M. Le Brun to Lord Grenville, Star, 22d May.

hostilities,

hoftilities, or her paffions gratified by the continuance of deftruction.

It is well known that the treaty of Pillnitz was the fource of all the prefent hoftilities; and it might have been forefeen that an attempt to carry it into effect would produce a great part of the calamities which have enfued. At the time that this took place, the conftitution of France was fettled; the king and the people had fworn to obey it. There was in it a good deal to praife, and much to blame; but, for reafons which it would be ufelefs to detail, it was on the whole impracticable. The men of talents and influence in France had however feen their error in weakening the executive power too much; they were rallying round the throne; and the army, headed by the pureft and moft popular character in the nation, were acquiring every day more and more military habits and virtues. The conftitution, with all its faults, had produced the moft fenfible advantages to the labouring part of the people *; it contained within itfelf the means of correcting both its principles and practice; and there was perhaps a chance that thefe might have been remedied without a civil war. It is however far more probable that a civil war muft have enfued; but if the parties had been left to themfelves, there is no one will deny that Fayette and his friends, in poffeffion of all the conftitutional authorities, would in all human probability have been victorious, and the ill-fated monarch have preferved his life and his crown. In the mean time the reft of Europe might have refted in peace—the conftitution, modelled perhaps on our own, would have affumed a more practicable and confiftent form, and liberty been eftablifhed on law.

The danger to which the final triumph of the new conftitution was expofed, arofe from a foreign war If the neigh-

* See the Tour of Mr. Arthur Young.

bouring

bouring nations fhould attempt an invafion of France for the
avowed purpofe of reftoring its ancient government, from
that inftant it was evident that the conftitution and the king
himfelf were in extreme hazard. By the conftitution, the whole
means of the nation's defence againft this invafion muft be
trufted in the hands of the king himfelf, to replace whom in
unlimited power the invafion was made. Among a people
intoxicated with liberty, and jealous in the extreme, it was
impoffible that any wifdom could in fuch circumftances fecure an already fufpected monarch from the imputation of
treachery. As the danger from this treachery became
greater, the paffions of the people arofe ; when the Duke of
Brunfwick entered France, they burft into open infurrection,
and through a fcene of dreadful flaughter the conftitution
was overturned, and the monarch dethroned. This crifis
was forefeen by the Jacobins, and by every means provoked ;
it was forefeen by the Feuillans (the true friends of liberty
and of limited monarchy), and earneftly deprecated. The
virtuous monarch himfelf was fenfible of his danger, and in
his extreme diftrefs applied to England to avert it. It was
evident that the Emperor would not venture on this invafion
without the aid of our ally the king of Pruffia, who had no
more pretence for attacking France, than for his invafion of
Poland, in which fuch flagrant wickednefs and fuch deteftable
hypocrify have been openly difplayed. The unhappy Louis
intreated our interference to detach the king of Pruffia from
his defign, in language the moft preffing and moft pathetic.
Such an opportunity of exerting great power on a moft fub-
lime occafion, and to the nobleft of purpofes, is not likely
to recur in a fingle age, and is referved by providence for its
choiceft favourites. Such an opportunity was prefented to
you, and you weakly and blindly caft it away.

The language which you put into your fovereign's
mouth on that occafion is on record.—Profeffing every good

wish for the king of France, mankind were then told, that
the king of England could not interfere, unless he was re-
quested by all the parties concerned; that is, not only by
him in distress, but by those also whose conduct occasioned
the danger! The conspirators at Pillnitz, and the Jacobins
of Paris, equally triumphed on this occasion.—The constitution and liberties of France were the objects of their common
attack. At the same instant foreign war and internal insur-
rection fell with all their furies on the friends of the king, of
law, and of order; the streets and the prisons of Paris over-
flowed with their blood; and those who escaped the daggers
of the Jacobins were seized on the frontier by our ally of
Pruffia, loaded with chains, and sent to the dungeon of Mag-
deburg, to perish in silence, or suffer in hopeless captivity
worse than death can inflict. Gratified in the destruction of
their common enemy, the votaries of superstition and of en-
thufiasm have met in dreadful conflict; a war of unexampled
fury has ensued; and after the sacrifice of a hundred thou-
sand lives, the flower of the youth of France and Germany,
the hostile armies are precisely in the same situation as when
the carnage began!

Another opportunity had in the mean time offered for
England to interfere, and to restore the peace of Europe.—
Winter produced a temporary suspension of hostilities. It
is well known that Pruffia, baffled and worn out, wished, during this armistice, to make its peace with France, and that
Spain was about to settle its difference with her also. Auftria, left alone, was unequal to the contest, and by our media-
tion peace might have been restored.—Difficulties had indeed
occurred: France had not only repelled her invaders, but
had in her turn become the aggressor, and Flanders had been
over-run by the arms of the victorious republic. The pof-
fession of Flanders by France might not only weaken Austria
too much (I use the language of politicians), but expofe Holland

land to be invaded and over-run—France muſt therefore be induced to renounce Brabant. In the mean time there were new difficulties in the way of negociating with France, from the change which had taken place in its government. Thoſe who had hardly been able to ſee with patience the repreſentative of the conſtitutional king, could not be expected to receive with kindneſs the delegate of the new republic. If however we treated at all, it muſt be with thoſe who held the reins of government, men, it muſt be acknowledged, againſt whom the feelings of almoſt every heart in England revolted. A miniſter is, however, to conſult his reaſon, not his feelings, and to liſten only to the intereſts of his country. If theſe require peace, his duty is to procure it by every fair and reaſonable means; and, if he treats at all, to treat with temper, even though his opponents are *robbers in their cave*. If war, on the other hand, be inevitable, his buſineſs is evident—to refuſe all negociation, and to let looſe the whole force of the ſtate. You took a middle courſe: the dangers of war could not be altogether overlooked. You would treat therefore, but under a delicate diſtinction, which was to appear to our allies as if we did not treat at all; and, as it ſhould ſeem, to ſecure your honour, you ſet out in the buſineſs with *refuſing the right of your antagoniſts to hold a treaty*. Le Brun and his aſſociates however ſubmitted; it is known that they were ready to have renounced Brabant, rather than go to war with England; and univerſal peace was perhaps once more in your power. By this time however the nation was inflamed to a great degree by the apprehenſion of internal conſpiracies; and the dreadful anathemas of Mr. Burke in the houſe of commons had deſtroyed all temper and moderation. From Mr. Fox the mention of peace with France had been received almoſt with execration, and England was pervaded with the ſpirit of the ancient cruſades. In this ſituation every moment became more critical—you heſitated—negociation

was

was one day begun and the next abandoned—Standing on the brink of a precipice, you dallied with the temper of two inflamed nations, and were pushed forwards into this bloody war. If you did not act as a great statesman on this occasion, some apology may be found for you—your temper was perhaps irritated; your sense of honour and your feelings of sympathy outraged; and though the minister cannot be pardoned, the man may stand excused. Deeply as I lament the war and its consequences, I must fairly admit, that the madness of the moment renders it doubtful, whether it could have been avoided during the last days of negociation, by any measures in your power. Indecision is certainly not a part of your character in seasons of difficulty or danger; but on this occasion it seems fairly to be imputed to you; and to this it was owing that the *alarmists* had taken the nation out of your hands.

Without imputing bad motives to those who stood forward to propagate the rumours of internal sedition and conspiracy on that occasion, it may now, I think, be said pretty confidently, that their fears greatly magnified the real danger. Why they were terrified, and why their terrors were in a great measure vain, may be easily understood by any one acquainted with human nature, who looks at all the events of that period with an impartial eye. The retreat of the Duke of Brunswick, the battle of Jemappe, and the conquest of Flanders came so rapidly and so unexpectedly upon us, that men who had blindly wished, and weakly predicted, the immediate subjugation of France to the Prussian arms, were seized with a sudden terror proportioned to their foolish hopes. France, marching with giant strides over her frontier, seemed to threaten the world. Those who in the first instance had not taken into their calculation the force of enthusiasm acting on a great and powerful nation in a moment of external invasion, could not, it may reasonably be supposed, form any

just

juſt opinion of its nature or extent ; and ſaw in their fright-
ened imaginations, not only the downfall of the deſpotic
governments of Europe, but the overthrow of our own happy conſtitution, the ſource of ſo many bleſſings, and the well-
earned purchaſe of more than one revolution, and of many
years of civil war. On the other hand, the ſurpriſing ſucceſs of the French raiſed to a high elevation of ſpirits all
thoſe who, from whatever motives, had intereſted themſelves
in their favour; and the claſſic grace with which the ſpear
of Liberty was wielded at Jemappe, threw a momentary veil
over former proceedings, too foul to bear the light. In this
ſituation of things, it was impoſſible that parties feeling ſo
differently ſhould not be mutually offenſive to each other,
and that thoſe who triumphed for the moment ſhould not
become ſubjects of apprehenſion to thoſe already ſo dread-
fully alarmed.

During this ſtate of jealous fear, ſtrong confirmations
could not be wanting, for " trifles light as air" would have
ſerved the purpoſe ; and it is well known, that even the very
looks of the ſuppoſed republicans were ſtated in the houſe
of commons as proofs of their ſeditious views. It muſt however be acknowledged, that there were great folly and indiſ-
cretion, to ſay no worſe, in the conduct of many of the *new
Whigs* * ; and that the addreſſes to the National Aſſembly
from ſocieties in England, however they might be intended,
were incapable of producing any good, and were pregnant with
the moſt ſerious evils. Whether any thing reſembling a plot
really exiſted, cannot perhaps be as yet aſcertained. Floating
notions of change probably pervaded the imaginations, and
occaſionally eſcaped the lips of enthuſiaſts; but it does not
appear at all likely that any plan for this purpoſe was con-

---

* This deſcription of men has not yet got a name that both they and their
opponents admit—Patriots and Jacobins are the party deſignations—I chooſe
a middle term, and quote for this appellation the authority of Mr. Burke.

cerred

certed or even meditated in any quarter. And the notion fo
induftrioufly circulated, that there was among us a large body
of men, fome of them of the firft talents, leagued in a con-
fpiracy againft their country with the Jacobin party of France,
is one of thofe wild and " foolifh things," of which in a few
months thofe who credited it " will in their cooler moments
be afhamed," and which will foon be remembered only for
mifchief it has done.

It is to this general fufpicion that the war itfelf is in
great meafure to be attributed. One part of the cabinet, as
report fays, was warmly and decidedly for it from the firft ;
and the eagernefs of the *Alarmifts* in the houfe of commons
in favour of this bloody meafure is well known. A ftep fo
fatal to the general interefts of the country would not, however, have been taken in the face of even a feeble oppofition
out of doors. Three public meetings—at Manchefter, Wake-
field, and Norwich, prevented the Ruffian war. But where
was oppofition now to come from ? Every man that objected
to a meafure of minifters was by this time fuppofed to be an
enemy to the conftitution ; and he who oppofed a war with
France, was openly cried down as a fecret ally of the Jacobins,
and as only anxious to fave them from the force of our irre-
fiftible arm. Profeffions of attachment to our own happy
conftitution were regarded as of no value, unlefs they were
accompanied with a blind and unlimited confidence in adminiftration ; and he only was confidered as a true friend to his
country, who was ready to put all our bleffings at hazard, by
rufhing madly forward into this foolifh crufade.

The whole body that affociated with Mr. Reeves feemed
to think the fupport of the war neceffary to the fupport of
the conftitution ; and in the houfe of commons Mr. Burke,
with the peculiar phrenfy that diftinguifhes all his conduct,
reiterated the war-hoop of *atheifm*, and pronounced Mr. Fox's
propofal of attempting to avert hoftilities by negociation, as

a ftep

a ſtep that would by neceſſary conſequence expoſe our virtuous monarch, with little proſpect of eſcape, to the fate of
the unfortunate Louis *.

It was owing I preſume to the ſyſtem you have adopted,
that though, as it has ſince appeared, you were at this time
actually negociating, you preſerved a cautious ſilence, and
ſuffered the nation to believe you thought with Mr. Burke.
For the firſt time in his life Engliſhmen were in ſympathy
with this extraordinary character, and madneſs became more
contagious than the plague.

If it were at all proper to argue with men who can believe that the only means of ſecuring the reverence of the nation for the conſtitution, is to plunge us into all the horrors
and miſeries of a foreign war, I would point out the conſequences that may poſſibly reſult from the rebound of general
ſentiment, from the union of ſtarving ignorance with deſperate ambition, and from the progreſs of poverty, miſery,
and diſcontent. But I do not think it neceſſary at preſent to
inſiſt on ſuch topics ; becauſe, blindly and fooliſhly as ſuch
men have acted on their own principles, I believe the ſeaſon

---

* The manner in which this ſtrange man has introduced his ſovereign
into debate, at different times, is truly curious. His conduct in this reſpect
during the regency, when he repreſented the Almighty as *having hurled him
from his throne*—and at the time now alluded to, when, in the exceſs of his loy-
alty, he expreſſed his fears *of his being beheaded*—are apparently much con-
traſted, but evidently flow from the ſame ſtructure of mind. A man that
could talk openly in the houſe of commons of the " king's head being cut
off," is not, however, I apprehend, likely to be appointed a lord of the
bed-chamber, or even a gentleman-uſher. Mr. Burke, it is ſaid, is a poet ;
and this is true. But there ſeems about him a phreaſi that is more than
poetical—an habitual diſpoſition to exaggeration, that treſpaſſes the bounds,
not of truth only, but of nature—and an irritability that has no reſemblance
to any thing to be ſeen in rational life, and that impreſſes upon us the notion of a *mind diſeaſed !* In this view of the ſubject Mr. Burke is perhaps
an object of pity. When his fits are not upon him, he is known to be gen-
tle and humane.

of

of delufion is paffing, and that Englifhmen will be able to diftinguifh, under every event, the fubftantial excellence of our conftitution ; and attribute their fufferings, whatever they may be, to their own delufion, and the madnefs of thofe who have mifled the public mind.

But it may be faid that the war is likely to be fhort and fuccefsful, and is therefore now to be perfifted in, however indifcreetly it may have been begun.

The anfwer to this is not difficult—The war has had already all the fuccefs that we could hope for : it brought on the invafion of Holland, and that invafion is repelled : it has obl'ged the I rench to abandon Flanders—to do that by force, which they were before inclined to do by negociation : it has covered the fea with our fhips of war, and made the merchantmen both of France and England difappear—and finally, after feveral hard fought battles, it has enabled the king of Pruffia to lay fiege to Mentz, and the Prince of Coburg to fit down before Valenciennes—But what is really of importance, it has brought from the French new offers of peace.

What then may be the caufe why we fo proudly and fullenly (as it is faid) reject them ?

It may be faid, that we wifh to carry on the war till we obtain a barrier againft the future irruptions of the French into Holland or Brabant; and that, this being effected, we mean with our allies to reft on our arms, and leave the nation to fettle its own government. If this be our policy, it were far better to reft now.

The probability of obtaining and of preferving peace depends, in a great meafure, on the terms which are offered according with natural principles of equity. That every nation fhould keep within its own confines, and choofe its own government, without moleft..ng its neighbours, is a propofition which is agreeable to our common apprehenfions of juftice ; and, applied fairly and equally to the powers at war,

it

it may produce a ſpeedy and laſting peace. But to inſiſt, as a ground-work of ſuch a treaty, that the Auſtrians ſhall obtain and keep poſſeſſion of thoſe ſtrong fortreſſes on the northern frontier by which France is defended, is to propoſe that which is equally offenſive to the pride and alarming to the fears of Frenchmen, and which is likely to occaſion a vaſt and a fruitleſs effuſion of human blood. " Shall we conſent (they will cry) that France ſhall be diſmembered ? Shall we abandon our countrymen of Liſle and Valenciennes to the deſpots of Germany ? If we give up a part of our territory, what ſecurity ſhall we have that the dividers of Poland will reſt contented with a part, eſpecially when, by poſſeſſing our ſtrong holds, they may invade us at pleaſure, and march at once into the heart of our defenceleſs country ?" Such are the queſtions that will be aſked, and it muſt be acknowledged that they are founded on natural feelings and reaſonable fears : before theſe are ſubdued, many a brave man will periſh in the field. But if indeed the ſecurity of the Low Countries be our only object, why not fortify Namur, Mons, Tournay, &c. which the Emperor Joſeph diſmantled, under an idea (which illuſtrates very ſtrongly the folly of attempting to look far into futurity) that the marriage of his ſiſter with the unfortunate Louis would render a barrier needleſs on the ſide of France ? If thoſe fortifications which were thought ſufficient againſt Louis XIV. are not ſufficient againſt the proud republicans, why not erect others ? and if bankrupt Auſtria cannot do this, let us (if we muſt mingle in their affairs) be taxed to ſupport them, but let it be for an expenditure that will terminate in peace.

The real intereſt of foreign nations is not, whether France ſhall have a conſtitution of this or that form ; it is, that ſhe ſhall have a regular government of ſome form or other, which may ſecure the faith of treaties, and due ſubordination to law ; and this is the intereſt of the people of France themfelves more than any other. Why then, it may be faid, do they not follow their intereſt? Becauſe they do not perceive it; and they are prevented from perceiving it by the preſſure of external war.

Revolutions of government call forth great talents and virtues, but they alſo too frequently call forth great crimes. Where all the uſual ordinances of law and ſociety are broken down, men will riſe indeed in ſome degree according to their activity and powers, but in a degree too according as theſe are exerted without ſcruple or reſtraint. In the enthuſiaſtic ſtate of mind by which revolutions are accompanied, great crimes make little impreſſion on the *million*, provided they are committed in the ſpirit of party, and under the appearance of patriotiſm. Compaſſion, charity, candour, and even a ſenſe of juſtice, are too generally ſwept away in the whirlwind of paſſion and prejudice, and lie buried under the wreck of virtuous habits and principles, to revive in quieter times. In ſuch a ſtate of things the natural influence of integrity and property, as well as the artificial diſtinctions of rank and birth, give way to the governing power of enthuſiaſm; and men often riſe to direction and command from the loweſt ſtations, by the force of ſtrong talents and bold tempers, and by the buoyancy of heated imaginations.

Enthuſiaſm is in ſeaſons of danger felt by virtuous as well as by unprincipled minds—by the former indeed perhaps more than the latter: but in virtuous minds, while it expands all the generous feelings, it does not deſtroy the reſtraints of principle or honour, even towards antagoniſts or enemies, and much leſs towards thoſe embarked in the ſame cauſe.

Revolutions however, in their progreſs, ſtir up ſociety more and more, even to the very dregs, and bring forward more and more of ignorance and profligacy (terms which in political life are nearly convertible) into the general maſs of

feeling

feeling and of action, in which the national will and the national force refide. Men who wifh to guide this will, and direct this force, in times of popular commotion, muft partake of its character, and vary their conduct with the rapid changes which the general fentiment undergoes. But in every great revolution this fentiment has a tendency to become gradually worfe, and the character of thofe at the helm muft become worfe alfo. In the courfe of this melancholy progrefs, therefore, men of real principle and pure honour, who cannot bend to the opinions of the day, are probably thrown off, or perhaps deftroyed, and are fucceeded by other defcriptions, each in fucceffion more unlike the firft, till at laft perhaps the unprincipled and defperate obtain undifputed fway.

Hence, in our own country, the refiftance to Charles I. which was led by Hampden and Faulkland, terminated in Cromwell and Lambert: and hence the revolution of France, originating with Fayette, Neckar, and Mirabeau, has defcended into the hands of Danton and Roberfpierre *.

The

---

* The American revolution may be inftanced as an exception to this general reprefentation, but improperly. We muft firft obferve (as was noticed by Mr. Fox in his fpeech on Mr. Gray's motion) that in America, though there was a change of the governing power, there was no revolution of habits or opinions—no fudden change of principles. It muft be obferved alfo, that the Americans had much lefs of poverty and ignorance among them (though lefs knowledge no doubt) than what is to be found in England and France. And thirdly, it muft be obferved, that fomething of the fame kind did actually take place in America as in England and France, though certainly in a lefs degree. Round the American Revolution, as well as the American character, a falfe glare has been thrown by the fplendour of their fuccefs. The congrefs did not, like the national affembly, expofe their debates and diffentions to their own people, much lefs to all Europe; but it is well known that a party prevailed in it to a confiderable degree, and Washington himfelf, if report fpeaks truth, was at one time preferved in his command by a fingle vote only. In the courfe of the revolution many bloody deeds were acted, the memory of which need not now be revived. But the

The influence however of men who openly violate the firft obligations, as well as the moft palpable interefts of fociety, is expofed to continual danger from the very fcaffolding on which it is raifed, and cannot furvive that heated and enthufiaftic ftate of mind which extinguifhes for a time, and for a time only, the feelings of compaffion and the fenfe of juftice.

Enthufiafm is, from its very violence, of fhort continuance : it produces the moft cruel defolations in fociety : but, as Mr. Hume has obferved, " its fury is like that of thun- " der and tempeft, which exhauft themfelves in a little time, " and leave the air more calm and ferene than before." The accounts that we receive of the French fhew clearly, that they are at prefent a nation of enthufiafts : of this their very crimes give the moft decided evidence. Their contempt of danger and hardfhips ; their utter difregard of felf-intereft, and of all the motives which influence men in tranquil life ;

---

following quotation from the hiftory of the American revolution by Dr. Ramfay, himfelf a member of the congrefs, will fhew how the morals of the people were affected, and bear teftimony to the author's candour and love of truth. " Time and induftry have already, in a great degree, repaired the loffes of " property which the citizens fuftained during the war, but both have " hitherto failed in effacing the taint which was then communicated to " their principles ; nor can its total ablution be expected ti'l a new gene- " ration arifes, unpractifed in the iniquities of their fathers." If indeed Dr. Ramfay had not acknowledged this, the conduct of the affemblies which were elected immediately after the revolution would fufficiently prove it. By thefe affemblies ftanding on a popular bafis (efpecially by that of South Carolina) acts were paffed diffolving the obligations of juftice in a way as arbitrary, and nearly as open, as thofe of the moft defpotic monarch whatever. An experience of the evils refulting from fuch outrages has reformed both the principles and the practice of the American politicians ; and men of honour and integrity, many of them beaten down by the revolution, have recovered their proper influence in quieter times. Over and above all the circumftances I have mentioned, the natural phlegm of the American character, compared with the vehemence and impetuofity of the French, was an advantage not to be calculated.

their

their frantic fchemes; their wild fufpicions; their implaca-
bility towards their enemies; their pronenefs to murder;—
thefe are the true and exact features of enthufiafm, operat-
ing on minds previoufly degraded by a fuperftition the moft
vile, and by a flavery the moft abject *.

The more fiercely this national difeafe rages, the more
certainly will it terminate fpeedily, provided it be left to itfelf. Society cannot poffibly fubfift under the prefent fyftem
in France, and the exceffes of the Jacobins muft fooner or
later produce their deftruction. The nation, waking from
its delirium, will fee the horror of its fituation, and fly for a
refuge from anarchy to the conftitution it has rejected, or fome
better regulated form of government; or perhaps to the very
defpotifm it has overthrown. But, if continued attacks are
made from without, this iffue will certainly be prolonged,
and may perhaps be prevented, till the defpotic governments
now in arms, every day becoming more poor, and therefore
more oppreffive, fhall be themfelves brought to the ground!

The great inftrument of the fuccefs of the Jacobins has
been the fufpicion they have conftantly excited, that every
friend of peace and fubordination was connected with the
foreign enemies that are invading France †. A high-fpirited
nation will not receive the pureft of bleffings on compulfion,

---

* In Dr. Moore's Journal, various proofs of the truth of this may be
found.—A Sans Culotte prefenting to the National Affembly, on the 10th of
Auguft, the head of a murdered Swifs, and at the fame time emptying out of
his hat the jewels and gold which he had found in the Thuilleries, is a ftrik-
ing picture of the fpecies of difeafe of mind under which the nation labours.

† The ftrength of fuch an inftrument as this may be judged of by the
fuccefs with which it was employed by the *alarmifts* here. The friends of
peace in this country were in the fame manner denounced as leagued with
foreign invaders; and this was the real fecret of Meffrs. Reeves, Burke, and
Co. for *levelling the levellers*, at the fuccefs of which, confidering the men,
many people have been fo much furprifed. The nation was panic-ftruck,
and apprehenfion and credulity go hand in hand.

and

and would reject the British constitution itself, though it were absolutely perfect, if presented on the bayonet's point. But what boon do the conquerors of Poland hold out to them? What blessings do the people of Germany offer to their view? Absolute subjugation to a foreign force is the favour and the mercy of the rulers; ignorance and submission to unlimited oppression is the example of the armed slaves whom they command. It is no wonder that a nation of enthusiasts should be inflamed to madness on the approach of such invaders, and, spurning the dictates of reason, should consider those who would restrain them as leagued with their enemies, and commit themselves to such only as are as frantic as themselves. Hence every attempt to restore order to France has been frustrated by foreign invasion; Clermont-Tonnerre and Rochfoucauld have been murdered; and Narbonne, Fayette, and Liancourt have fled. And hence also it is but too likely that the siege of Valenciennes and Condé will prove the ruin of the brave and perhaps honest insurgents on the banks of the Loire. How certain the overthrow of the Jacobin system in France would be, if the nation were left to itself, may be gathered, not only from the nature of that system, but from the attempts to overturn it in the very face of a foreign invasion; and how very unlikely the allies are to succeed in their endeavours to give a constitution to France by force (the only rational object for which war can be continued), may be collected, not only from the history of the past, and from what has been already mentioned, but from other considerations.

Under the pressure of external invasion, almost any government will hold a nation together; and every form of republican government, however unfit for quieter seasons, is at such times productive of great energy of mind, and therefore of great national force. The cause of this is to be traced to the peculiar consequence which a republican government

gives

gives to the individual, by which his country becomes of confequence to him, and the whole ftrength of his private and public affections in a moment of external invafion bears on a fingle object—the national defence. The truth of this might be amply illuftrated from the hiftory of the republics of Greece and Rome; where may be feen alfo, what appears fo very extraordinary in modern times, the moft unbounded licentioufnefs and confufion in the centre of the government, joined with the moft formidable power on the frontiers*.

In times of peace the exiftence of primary affemblies, fuch as are univerfal in France, feems incompatible with the fafety of eftablifhed government; but in a fituation like the prefent, thefe will be the nurferies of courage, of eloquence, of daring minds;—by giving every individual an active and perfonal intereft in the ftate, they will ftrengthen its defence in an extraordinary manner. The divifion of France into diftricts and departments, eftablifhes within it fo many rival republics, and in this way will probably produce that high-fpirited emulation between neighbouring communities, fo dangerous to internal quiet, but to which Greece, when invaded, owed its fafety in the claffic ages, and perhaps Switzerland its independence in modern times.

In the progrefs of revolutions, it is material to obferve, that talents do not feem to fuffer an equal degradation with principles. On the contrary, fituations of continued difficulty and danger have a tendency to call them forth (in as far as

---

* In this refpect, as well as in feveral others, France recalls to our minds the ftates of antiquity. There are indeed circumftances of refemblance in their fituation that might afford room for much curious obfervation, and our hefitation in applying the experience we derive from Greece or Rome to modern France is perhaps chiefly founded on a doubt, which at times has appeared reafonable enough—whether thefe countries have contained beings of the fame fpecies—whether thefe French be indeed men, or fome other defcription of animals.

they

they are diftinct from virtue) more and more, and to
ftrengthen and expand them when found. In long eftablifhed monarchies, fuch as are fpread over the continent of
Europe, rank has the chief, or indeed the fole influence in
beftowing command, and nature in beftowing talents pays
no attention to rank. But in revolutions, artificial diftinctions being overturned, the order of nature is in fome degree
reftored, and talents rife to their proper level. Hence it is
that revolutions, once fet on foot, have the weight of talents
generally in their favour. It may be objected, indeed, that
when the fword is once drawn, the iffue depends on military
difcipline and fkill, and that thefe will always be found on
the fide of experience. Daily obfervation however proves,
that the mere mechanifm of a foldier is eafily and fpeedily
learnt; and the uniform voice of hiftory tells us, that the
qualities of a great general are in an efpecial manner the
work of nature; what fuperior genius feems to acquire the
fooneft, and what all other men find it impoffible to acquire
at all. Hence, though in the beginning of wars difcipline
and eftablifhed rank have ufually the advantage, in the courfe
of them nature and genius always preponderate *.

* The whole of thefe obfervations might be illuftrated from our own
civil wars. Deteftable as Cromwell and his affociates were in many refpects,
they muft be allowed to have poffeffed very fuperior talents both in the cabinet and the field. In the beginning of the war, military experience was
entirely with the king; but, what is curious, there did not arife one good com-
mander on his fide, the gallant Montrofe excepted, and he, it may be obferved, was educated among the covenanters. On the other fide arofe Effex,
Fairfax, Cromwell, Ireton, Lambert, and Monk. Moft of thefe had no previous acquaintance with military affairs. Cromwell, the firft captain of the
age, was forty-three years old before he became a foldier. Thefe curious
circumftances have not efcaped Mr. Hume, nor the explanation of them.
Reflecting on this fubject, I have fometimes amufed myfelf with fuppofing
what fort of military commanders our political leaders would make, and I
apprehend they would arrange themfelves pretty much according to their
prefent order.—Firft-rate talents are of univerfal application.

The

The application of thefe obfervations to the affairs of France is fo obvious, that it would be fuperfluous, as well as tedious, to point it out.

The impoffibility of conquering opinions by the fword, and the dreadful flaughter which the attempt when perfifted in muft neceffarily occafion, may be learnt from the revolution in the Low Countries, and the bloody tranfactions which were there carried on under the direction of Alva. If the great mafs of the people have imbibed opinions, extermination only can root them out. Hence the *fundamentality* of the French revolution, fo much exclaimed againft by the weak and fearful, and fo much dreaded even by the enlightened, though it will probably be the fource of long internal diffentions, renders it invulnerable by foreign attack. Mr. Hume has remarked the univerfal and extreme reluctance with which men abandon power once poffeffed; and you, Mr. Pitt, can probably fpeak to this truth from your own feelings.—Well then, Sir, the Sans Culottes have recovered what they call their rights, and may be faid to be men in power—power newly tafted, after long and hard oppreffion. Whether this power be good for them or not is another thing—they think it good, and that is enough. When once they have obtained quiet poffeffion of it, they will probably abufe it, as other men in power have done before them. But while it is attempted to be wrefted from them by armed force, it will rife every moment in their eftimation, and death only will be able to rob them of their prize. The revolution of Poland, on the other hand, was not a *fundamental* revolution; and it was praifed by Mr. Burke (a fufpicious circumftance) on this account. The truth is, it was a change of the form of government, and a partial enlargement of its bafis, from which however nine tenths of the people of Poland were entirely fhut out. When the king and the nobles therefore abandoned it, the peafantry abandoned

abandoned it alfo, and found no motive for rifking their lives in defence of bleffings they had not been permitted to tafte. This is the real caufe of the rapid fuccefs of the confederate arms, and not the open plains and difmantled fortreffes of the country, as fome have fuppofed. The true defence of a nation in fuch circumftances—the only defence that is impregnable, lies in the poor man's heart;—that abandoned, the reft is eafy.

In viewing this fubject, fo many confiderations rufh on the mind to fhew the folly of the prefent invafion of France, that I am compelled to dwell on general topics only; otherwife I might expatiate on the utter incapacity of the Auftrian army to keep the field at all without fupplies from this country, and the impoffibility of our finding fuch fupplies. Abject as the temper of the nation appears, it will not, I apprehend, fubmit to utter ruin; and I pronounce coolly, what I have confidered deeply, that nothing but utter ruin can be the confequence of our perfifting in this copartnerfhip with the folly and bankruptcy of the continental powers. It is not enough that we pay with Englifh guineas, extracted from the labour of our oppreffed peafantry, the people of Heffe and Hanover, to fight German battles; we muft fupport the armies of Auftria alfo, and, from the wreck of our ruined manufactures, fupply them with food, clothing, and arms. But what confummates our misfortunes is, that if by our affiftance the confederates fhould fucceed in their views, England will be blotted out of the fyftem of Europe: Holland cannot preferve her independence a fingle day; a connected chain of defpotifm will extend over the faireft portion of the Earth; and the lamp of Liberty, that has blazed fo brightly in our "Sea-girt Ifle," muft itfelf be extinguifhed in the univerfal night *.

The

* I purpofely avoid enlarging on this view of the fubject, becaufe I think nothing

The mifchief that is meditated is of a magnitude that feems more than mortal, but happily the execution of it requires more than mortal force. The ignorant and innocent flaves that are the inftruments on this occafion are men —they muft be clothed and fed—they have men to contend with, and are liable to the death they are fent to inflict—they may perifh by the fword, by fatigue, by famine, and by difeafe. The new Alarics that employ them are men alfo, weak, ignorant, and mortal like the reft. Death will foon level them with the inftruments of their guilty ambition. In a few years, or perhaps a few months, Catherine will fleep, lifelefs, with Jofeph, with Leopold, with *Peter the Third*. New characters lefs tinctured with prejudice will receive a portion of the fpirit of the age, the fyftems of defpotifm be broken, and mortality come in aid of reafon and truth.

In the mean time it is poffible that Condé and Valenciennes may be taken, and that the hoftile armies may march into France as before. If purfued into their own country, Frenchmen will, in all probability, continue united; and they will carry on the war, when compared to their affailants, at little expenfe. The men are on the fpot; their provifions are behind them; mufkets are in their hands; enthufiafm in their hearts. The more the nation is compreffed within its centre, the more will the elafticity of its force and courage increafe. The invaders will probably be again compelled to retreat, and their retreat will neither be eafy nor certain: the victorious republicans will purfue them, and again, perhaps, difdaining the reftraints of prudence, pufh their conquefts to the banks of the Rhine. A fingle action loft, a fingle action recovered, Flanders; and Flanders and Holland will now feel the fame blow.

nothing fo unlikely as the conqueft of France. It has been difcuffed in the Morning Chronicle, by a writer under the fignature of " A Calm Obferver," with a perfpicuity and force of reafoning that nothing can furpafs. The whole feries of letters far exceed any fimilar production of the Englifh prefs.

What

What shall save Holland if Flanders fall? The Cold-stream you see are mortal men. Even the three princes of the blood-royal of England will not appal the fierce republicans—*What care these roarers for the name of King* * ? If the danger I state seems at a distance, let it not on that account be disregarded. Every step the allied armies advance into France, the danger seems to me to approach; and were they within ten leagues of Paris, I should tremble the more for the fate of Amsterdam.

The opportunity of restoring general peace presented itself at the time of the congress of Antwerp. Dumourier had retreated; Flanders was recovered. We had nothing to do but to declare, what must I think be declared in the end, that *if France will confine herself within her own territory, she may there shape out her own constitution at her will.* Had this been done at the time mentioned, Dumourier, not rendered odious by foreign alliance, would in all probability have been able to restore the constitutional monarchy; and in every event, France, occupied by intestine divisions, would, as it seems probable, have left Europe in quiet for many years to come. This policy was so clear that a mere child might have discerned it; it did not even require a negociation with the French cabinet, and while it secured our best interests, it left our honour without a stain.

How then shall we account for the resolves of the congress of Antwerp? We must unveil the truth. The members of this congress were German princes, or their agents; even the representative of England there *was a German prince.* Such men, from their education, are in general ignorant, and labour under prejudices, from their situation, of a destructive kind.

Military despots in their own dominions, they feel it their personal interest, perhaps they think it the interest of mankind (such may be the force of prejudice) that despotism should be univerfal. To fuch men the anarchy of France, under Jacobin rulers, is not half fo alarming as the conftitution to which this may give birth. They are aware that the crimes acting there at prefent are fufficient to render the French name deteftable among their fubjects ; but if thefe crimes fhould open the eyes of the French themfelves—if, out of the mingled wrecks of defpotifm and anarchy, a limited monarchy ſhould arife in France, as it did in England, or any other form of a free conftitution that fecures fubordination to law—then it is that the French example will become far more deftructive to arbitrary governments than their arms, and the crowned heads of Germany, great and fmall, will have real caufe to tremble. It is true, if they were enlightened, they need not tremble at all ; they would fee that arbitrary power is as deftructive to him that poffeffes, as to him that endures it. But it cannot be expected that they fhould difcern this— the errors of education blind all but very fuperior minds ; and though Germany produces more princes than all Europe befides, it is not once in a century that fhe produces a prince that is a truly great man*.

Mr. Fox contends that government is *from* the people ; Mr. Wyndham that it is only *for* the people. Thefe philological diftinctions are not attended to by the rulers of Germany, among whom even the word *people* is not to be found. Their *fubjects*, they know, are accuftomed to obedience ; the bleff-

* Frederick the Second was an extraordinary man, and it has amufed many perfons to fuppofe how he might have acted on the prefent occafion. This however feems pretty certain, that he would not have lain eight months in the neighbourhood of Mentz before he found an opportunity of laying fiege to it. The prefent conduct of the Pruffians conveys an eulogium on the talents of that great monarch, beyond the power of Hertzberg's oratory. As however they confidered themfelves facrificed before, their prefent backwardnefs may arife as much from fpleen as from any other caufe.

ings

ings that flow from liberty and property they have never ex‐
perienced, and they are therefore fit inftruments in the hands
of arbitrary power.   Germany, it is well known, is inhabited
chiefly by princes, nobles, muficians, and peafantry ; mer‐
chants, manufacturers, and country gentlemen, the leading
defcriptions of Englifhmen, are there almoft wholly un‐
known.   The three firft of thefe claffes are, during war,
in their natural element ; and the laft, who fuftain all the evils
and all the burthens, are as yet too abject and too ignorant
to make their fufferings dangerous to thofe by whom they are
opprefifed.   A perfeverance in the war will indeed deftroy
what little trade and manufactures there are in Germany, and
render their governments (that of Hanover excepted, whofe
military expenfes are defrayed by England) univerfally bank‐
rupt.   The creditors of the ftates will be ruined, but the ex‐
penfes of the courts and armies will not perhaps on that
account be lefs.   The ordinary revenue of a German
prince depends chiefly on the products of the foil, and
dreadful muft be the oppreffion indeed, before thefe fail.   The
peafantry will be taxed more and more to fupport increafing
burthens, and the extortion of fuch taxes will rivet the po‐
verty and ignorance through which alone thefe burthens are
endured.   It is thus that the tyranny of the rulers and the
degradation of the people muft keep equal pace ; it is thus
that defpotifm forms a natural alliance with ignorance,
blafts every charm of rational nature, and blunts every
feeling of the human heart.   There is indeed a point
at which the oppreffion of the moft abject becomes no
longer fafe — a point to which, if I miftake not, the defpotic
governments of Europe are faft approaching.   They have
undertaken to fubdue the enemies of kingly government in
France, and are ftaking their whole credit on the iffue of an
undertaking from which, according to every human appearance,
they will return baffled and difgraced.   The moft defpotic
governments

7

governments depend for their exiſtence on opinion, as well as the moſt free. If the concert of princes ſhould be baffled, the prejudices of their ſubjects will be ſhaken, and the foundation of their thrones will from that moment be for ever inſecure.

Behold then, once more, a criſis which has ſo often occurred in hiſtory; which has preſented ſo frequent and ſo awful a warning to rulers, and has preſented it ſo often in vain! A government bankrupt by its own waſte and folly; ſenſible of its inſecurity, and therefore jealous, irritable, and oppreſſive. A people already labouring under almoſt intolerable burthens, and doomed to ſuffer others more heavy ſtill—caſting off, with its prejudices, the habitual ſubmiſſion and reſpect to its rulers, and imbibing thoſe immutable truths which are ſo dangerous to oppreſſors, and ſometimes indeed ſo fatal to thoſe who are oppreſſed. Every day the breach widens—the ſword at length is drawn, and the ſcabbard caſt away.—In the dreadful conflict which follows there is only one alternative; the government muſt be overturned, or the people reduced to the condition of beaſts. We cannot have forgotten the cauſes which have produced the revolutions of Switzerland, Holland, and England—which have ſo recently produced the revolution of France;—the ſame cauſes are again conſpiring to ſhake all Europe to its centre, and to form a new æra in human affairs.

What a dreadful infatuation is it which involves the fate of Engliſhmen in this impending ruin—which embarks our commerce, our manufactures, our revenue, perhaps our conſtitution itſelf, the ſource of all our bleſſings, in this deſperate cruſade of deſpotiſm and ſuperſtition againſt anarchy and enthuſiaſm! in the courſe of which, however it terminate, we can reap nothing but misfortune; and in the iſſue of which we may learn, that no human inſtitution can withſtand the folly of thoſe who adminiſter its powers.

Men

Men of Switzerland, how I refpect you ! While the hurricane of human paffions fweeps over France, Italy, and Germany, elevated on your lofty mountains, you are above the region of the ftorm. Secure in your native fenfe, your fincere patriotifm, your fimple government, your invincible valour, your eternal hills—you can look down on the follies and the crimes which defolate Europe, with calmnefs and with pity, and anticipate the happy æra when perhaps you may mediate univerfal peace. Sea-girt Britain might have en-joyed this fituation, had fhe known how to eftimate her bleff-ings, and kept aloof from the madnefs of the day.

At this moment the feffion of parliament clofes ;—a dead ftillnefs prevails over England, the natural confequence of aftonifhment at the fpreading deftruction, and of ftrong paffions violently fuppreffed. The Oppofition, deferted by all thofe *feeble amateurs* whofe minds have not fufficient com-prehenfion to difcern the true intereft of their country, or whofe nerves are too weak to bear up againft vulgar prejudice, has endeavoured, but in vain, to difcover the extent of our continental engagements, or the real objects of the war *. Two hundred and eighty members, ranging behind you, fup-port every meafure you propofe ; and among the whole num-ber, not a man has been found to inquire of you openly, in the name and in behalf of the people of England, how long their patience is to endure, and how far the progrefs of ruin is to extend?

You have affumed on this awful occafion the whole re-fponfibility of public meafures, and your character and repu-tation, I fear, you miftakingly conceive, are wholly committed on the fuccefsful iffue of the war. Your real friends muft

---

* Security and compenfation are words that may be explained at pleafure.

fincerely

sincerely lament this on your own account ; the friends of
their country will lament it, on account of the general calamities it is likely to produce. The nation, Mr. Pitt,-has
loved you " well—not wisely;" and it is partly in consequence
of this that at the present moment her real interests are op-
posed to the personal honour of him she has trusted and ido-
lized. In this day of distress she is told to repose in the constitutional responsibility of ministers. " Be still, ye inhabi-
" tants of the isle, thou whom the merchants of Zidon that
" pass over the sea have replenished."—ISAIAH. Alas !
what will silence do ? Will the responsibility of ministers restore her ruined trade, feed her starving manufacturers ? will
it replace the husband and father to the widow or the orphan,
or restore to the aged parent his gallant son ? will it recall
to life the brave men now mouldering in unhallowed earth in
Flanders, joint-tenants of a common grave with those against
whom they fought* ?

* * * * * *

If I were bold enough to appreciate your political life,
Mr. Pitt, I should be inclined to allow the outset of it extraordinary merit. The sentiment of approbation that attended
you was indeed almost universal—you were the hope of the
good, the pride of the wise, the idol of your country. If your
official career had terminated with the discussions on the Regency, though one of the most fatal of your mistakes had
been committed before this, it may be questioned whether modern Europe could have produced a politician or an orator
more strenuous, more exalted, more authoritative†; one whose

---

* This affecting circumstance is, I am told, literally true.
† See Mr. Grattan's character of Lord Chatham, printed as Dr. Robertfon's.

ambition was apparently more free from felfifhnefs; who afforded to his opponents lefs room for cenfure, or gave to his friends more frequent occafions of generous triumph and honeft applaufe.—The errors that you have fallen into, are natural for men long poffeffed of power uncontrolled; and in imputing them to you, I accufe you only of the weak-neffes of human nature. It is not neceffary to a free people to have rulers exempt from fuch weakueffes; but it is necef-fary for them to watch and to guard againft thefe infirmities.

It is natural, I believe, for fuccefsful ambition to feek new objects on which it may exert itfelf. Hence, after you had fubdued oppofition in England, you iffued forth like another Hercules in queft of new adventures, and traverfed the continent of Europe to feek monfters whom you might fubdue. You could not however but be fenfible, that the reputation of a minifter of trade and finance, which you had juftly obtained, was incompatible with that of a great war minifter in the prefent ftate of the nation. You took therefore the middle line; you made preparations for fighting on every occafion, but you took care not to ftrike. England might perhaps bear the expenfe of arming, but could not actually go to war; and this fecret, which your three fucceffive armaments difcovered to all Europe, led Mirabeau on his death-bed to give you the name of *miniftre preparatif.*

In men long in poffeffion of power, a fecret fympathy (unknown perhaps to themfelves) is gradually ftrengthening in favour of others in the fame fituation, and a fecret pre-judice, amounting perhaps at laft to enmity, againft oppofi-tion to power in every form. Hence the danger you faw to England in the triumph of the patriots of Holland over the Prince of Orange, and the fafety we acquired from the fubjugation of the Dutch by the Pruffian arms.—Hence alfo the perfect compofure with which you expected the con-

queft

queſt of France by the deſpots of Germany, and the ſudden alarm with which you were ſeized, on the repulſion of that invaſion, and the overrunning of Flanders by the republican arms. By the freedom of Brabant the conſtitution of England might be endangered; but it became the more ſecure in your eye, it ſhould ſeem, by the extenſion of deſpotiſm over every corner of Europe, and the ſucceſs of foreign bayonets in rooting out *liberty* as well as licentiouſneſs in France.

It is alſo to the unhappy prejudices of your ſituation that I attribute your want of moderation of temper on occaſions of the utmoſt moment; your allying your great talents with the weak judgments and violent paſſions of thoſe around you ; and your blindneſs (if ſuch it be) to the real dangers of this commercial nation, and to the path of ſafety and of true honour, which it was no leſs your duty than your intereſt to purſue.

In contemplating events of ſuch magnitude as thoſe connected with the French revolution, the utmoſt calmneſs, as well as comprehenſion of mind, is required—and more particularly required in him who directs the affairs of a great nation. Unhappily theſe qualities are ſeldom found in any ſtation; and this revolution, ſeen in part only, has become the object of wild encomium, or of bitter reprobation, as the prejudices of men have been affected, or their ſympathies engaged. The moſt prudent part perhaps for one whoſe political ſituation is influenced by the opinions he is ſuppoſed to hold, is to be ſilent on the ſubject. It is uncertain how this extraordinary event may terminate, and its ultimate effects on the human race cannot yet be aſcertained. At preſent, however, it is well known, that not in England only, but in every part of Europe, the dreadful exceſſes in Paris, and elſewhere, have turned the tide of popular ſentiment and opinion ſtrongly againſt the French. Even under the moſt deſpotic governments, the people at preſent hug their chains, and

tyranny

tyranny itfelf is fecure. Can it then be fuppofed, that in
England there is any ferious danger from the contagion of
French principles; in England, where the conftitution is fo
fubftantially good, and the people fo loyal and united? The
theological and fectarian prejudices of different and oppofite
kinds through which the affairs of France have been viewed,
have indeed contributed moft fatally to bewilder the under-
ftanding, and to inflame the prejudices of Englifhmen; and
to thefe is to be imputed, in a great degree, that moft fingular
delufion—that the fafety of our conftitution has depended on
our rifking all our bleffings in this moft fruitlefs, expenfive,
and bloody war. That delufion (for fuch I confider it) is
now I hope nearly over; and peace, which is the general intereft, will foon, I doubt not, be the univerfal wifh. Every
confideration calls loudly for it; and it may be much more
eafily obtained now, when our enemies are humbled, and the
people of England are ftill patient and filent, than at a future
period, when the invading armies may be checked or repulfed,
and the nation is become openly impatient under the expenfe
and ruin of the war. A man of your fagacity will eafily difcern, that in times like the prefent, the gale of popular opinion is conftantly fhifting the point whence it blows, and
will fee that it cannot be trufted to carry you forward in your
prefent courfe, in the face of great and increafing obftacles.

The prefent ftate of affairs in this country, and on the
continent of Europe, forms a fubject too interefting to be left
without reluctance—but far too extenfive to be thoroughly
inveftigated within the limits of a letter like this. The
events of the day that is paffing are likely to affect every
portion of Europe, and, in their confequences, the condition
of the human race throughout the habitable earth. Many of
the "bearings and ties" of this important fubject I have been
obliged to neglect, and others I have only glanced at; for I
write on the fpur of the occafion, and under difficulties and

interruptions

interruptions of various kinds. Should what I have written have the fortune to reach you, you will fee that it is addreffed to you more " in forrow than in anger," and on that account alone that it is not wholly unworthy of your regard. But I would farther perfuade myfelf, that it may fuggeft topics for ferious reflection, by impreffing on your mind the progrefs and unexampled extenfion of the war-fyftem throughout Europe; the correfponding progrefs of the funding-fyftem; the crifis to which this laft has in fome countries reached, and is every where approaching; and the probable as well as certain effects of this on our own commercial nation, and on mankind at large.

Hitherto you have taken it for granted, that though there is a certain point of depreffion to which the commerce of this country may fink in confequence of the war, yet that from this, as in former wars, it will naturally return. I have fuggefted to you, that this fuppofition is dangerous, as well as fallacious, from the increafed progrefs of our debts and taxes, from the locking up of the capital of our manufacturers in foreign debts, and from the growing poverty as well as the general bankruptcy that fpreads over Europe, in confequence of the continued preffure of former burthens, and the unexampled extent and expenfe of the prefent war. I have not ftated to you, under this head, the effects of a rapidly finking revenue, or of the emigration of our people to America; becaufe thefe confiderations are fo extremely ferious that they cannot be mentioned without grief and alarm, and may form, of themfelves, a very ample fubject for feparate difcuffion.

Mr. Dundas told us, in the houfe of commons, that our commercial diftreffes arofe from our extraordinary profperity, and boafted that all the world united with us in the war againft France. I have fhewn that his affertion is a poor fophifm, and his boaft a fubject of forrow and apprehenfion.

Mr. Wyndham expreffed his acquiefcence in the lofs of

our

our commerce, if we might retain our conftitution; and on the fame ground of preferving our conftitution, this perilous war has been often defended by yourfelf, your followers, and a great part of the nation. I have made out to you, what I know not how, as chancellor of the exchequer, you can well be ignorant of, that our commerce and our conftitution have a moft intimate dependence on each other; and that when the union is formed by twenty-four millions of taxes, tythes, and poor-rates, and two hundred and fifty millions of debt, they may be confidered as embarked in the fame adventure, and as likely to perifh in the fame ftorm.

How the war commenced I have endeavoured to explain, and you will confider in your calmer moments, whether you really exerted yourfelf to preferve peace by negociation, inftead of procuring it by arms; and to what profit you have turned the honeft affection of your countrymen for their conftitution and king, and the generous indignation with which they furveyed the madnefs and brutality of their neighbours.

On various occafions during this bloody conteft I have fhewn that the peace of Europe was in our power; that it was in our power recently on the retreat of Dumourier, and after we ourfelves had tafted the calamities of war. Why it was rejected you muft yourfelf explain;—I have defcribed the congrefs at Antwerp, and am no farther mafter of the fubject.

The views that you conceal cannot be afcertained, but what you have actually performed is not liable to mif-apprehenfion. I have fuggefted to you, that you have united Englifhmen in the interefts and in the councils of thofe who formed the treaty of Pillnitz; who retain Fayette in chains; who were the real caufe of the triumphs of the Jacobin party in France over limited monarchy; who are in fact the pretext that the prefent anarchifts have

have employed, and will employ, to juftify their defperate
proceedings; and who, by their recent conduct in Poland,
have given fuch proofs of their ambition, as well as of their
power, as muft fill the heart of every friend of his fpecies
with horror and alarm. That the deftroyers of the conftitution of Poland can be friendly to our own, the model
on which it was formed, no one will believe. They are the
deadly foes of liberty throughout the world; and I might
have fhewn you, that in the deftruction of our revenue and
commerce, the bulwarks will be removed which fecure us
from their overwhelming force. I might alfo have pointed
out the danger of fending our army to fight under their ban-
ners, and our princes to affociate in their councils;—but
there are fentiments of ferious alarm which a lover of his
country muft deeply feel, that in this feafon of delufion it
may be dangerous to utter.

Of the two motives for continuing the war, fecurity and
compenfation, I have confidered that which alone I can un-
derftand, the former; and have fhewn that the attempt to
take and to feparate from France its frontier towns on the
north, is full of difficulty and hazard, and that while it may
render the war doubly bloody and defperate, it can afford
no fecurity beyond what might be obtained from fortifying
Auftrian Flanders, already in our power. The true fecurity
to this country arifing from the fettlement of the French government, I have endeavoured to fhew, is not promoted, but
abfolutely prevented by the prefent invafion, which, fhould it
be repelled, may leave unfortified Brabant, as well as Holland, an eafy conqueft to the republican arms.

In the fearful tragedy which is now acting on the theatre
of Europe, you have unhappily made England one of the perfons of the drama, and fhe cannot but act a part of unparalleled importance. You have affumed the direction of this

part

part to yourſelf, and before parliament again meets, the hopes and the fears of the enlightened, and the real intereſts of at leaſt the preſent race of mankind, may be at iſſue on your ſingle counſels. More than one falſe ſtep you have already made—the precipice is directly in your path, that leads to inevitable deſtruction. I know the temptations and the difficulties of your ſituation—we will forget the paſt, but if you advance, how ſhall you be forgiven ?

In conſidering the aſpect of the preſent times, I am ſometimes affected with deep melancholy; yet I am not one of thoſe who deſpair of the fortunes of the human race. Through the thick clouds and darkneſs that ſurround us, I diſcern the workings of an over-ruling mind. Superſtition I know is the natural offspring of ignorance, and governs in the dark ages with a giant's ſtrength.—Unaſſiſted reaſon is a feeble enemy : oppoſed to ſuperſtition, reaſon, in days of ignorance, is a dwarf. In the order of providence, enthuſiaſm ariſes to reſiſt ſuperſtition—to combat a monſter with a monſter's force. What did Eraſmus in the days of Luther ? What would Lowth have done in the days of Wycliffe, or Blair in thoſe of Knox ? In the councils of Heaven, mean and wicked inſtruments are often employed for the higheſt purpoſes. The authors of the reformation were many of them ignorant, fierce, and even bloody : but the work itſelf was of the moſt important and moſt univerſal benefit to the human race. The *deſpotiſm* of prieſts then received its death-wound, and the *deſpotiſm* of princes has now perhaps ſuſtained a ſimilar blow.—Pure religion has ſurvived and improved after the firſt ; the true ſcience of government may improve after the laſt, and be built every where on the ſolid foundations of utility and law. Before ſuch happy conſequences enſue, dreadful commotions may indeed be expected over Europe, commotions which England, and perhaps England only, may, if

the

she is wise, escape. The present generation will probably be swept away before the intellectual earthquake subsides; but those who succeed them, will, I trust, find the air more pure and balmy, and the skies more bright and serene.

June 6, 1793,

J. W.

POSTSCRIPT.

IN printing a fecond edition of this letter, it may not be ufelefs to enquire, how far the events which have happened fince its firft publication correfpond to the reprefentations, or illuftrate the reafonings, it contains.

Your warmeft and moft injudicious partizans, Mr. Pitt, will not de███that the bankrupt ftate of the continental powers, our ███s, becomes every day more evident.—Englihmen haye had a melancholy proof of the nature of the connections they have formed, not merely in the fubfidies to Hanover, or to that flower of chivalry the Prince of Heffe (who fells the lives of his fubjects at the rate of thirty banco crowns for each), but in the fuccours demanded by the Auftrians to enable them to keep the field; in the ruin of the commerce as well as the finance of Ruffia (when the ruble, by the regular operations of its government, is reduced, in foreign exchange, to lefs than half its value); and in that moft unprecedented of all treaties with the King of Sardinia, by which we are to pay him two hundred thoufand pounds annually, to keep up his own army, for the defence of his own country!

Though the merchants of this kingdom felt the fad effects of the war firft, it was predicted that on the manufacturers it would fall with the moft unrelenting ruin. The truth of this is now undeniable:—even the woollen and iron branches of manufacture, which in former wars in a great meafure efcaped, are now almoft in a ftate of ftagnation—He who handled the fhuttle for three fhillings a day, muft now take fixpence, and handle the fpear;—and many of the enlightened and virtuous affertors of the conftitution at Birmingham, fo fuccefsful in their fkirmifhes with herefy

and

and the beasts of the flesh, are now doomed to a harder service on the frontiers of France, where the " Bubble Reputation" must be " fought," not in the libraries or laboratories, or peaceful habitations of unprotected science, but in the hostile fortress, " and in the cannon's mouth."

The reasoning respecting paper-money is also confirmed—So far from this being the cause of our commercial distresses, it is now found, under proper regulations, to be the best alleviation for them that the times admit; and a Bank is proposed at Glasgow, and one has been established at Liverpool, for this express purpose.

What was observed on the subject of the supposed plots and conspiracies, which have so fatally bewildered the understandings of men, seems also to be strengthened by the progress of events.—The trial of Mr. Frost, from which so much was expected, is now before the public, and the tenderness of the recorder of Leicester has sunk deep into the public mind.—The zeal and activity of government have instituted various prosecutions, and leave no reason to suppose, that, through mistaken lenity, treason or sedition have been spared. As yet, however, the shadow of a conspiracy has not been discovered——If there be men, Mr. Pitt, lurking in the bosom of their country, who have plotted with France for the destruction of our constitution, let their guilty blood stream on the scaffold; the minister, who would spare them, is himself a traitor—but let not the friends of their king and country, who oppose your present measures, be involved in so foul a charge, " to fright the isle from its propriety," and to involve Us still deeper in this ruin and war.

With regard to those men who have persuaded themselves, that the safety of England depends on her persisting in the invasion of France, till monarchy shall be forced on that kingdom by the allied arms; the occurrences of the last two months on the continent may abate their confidence, and difpofe them to regard, with more attention and alarm, our fituation at home—The fearful diminution of our exifting revenue, and the increafed expenfes of the war, will require, it is evident, new methods and objects of taxation :—thefe our wounded commerce and our diminifhed confumption cannot poffibly fupport; and the neceffity of increafing the land tax is already incurred. But if the war continues, eight fhillings in the pound will do little towards the fupport of the public expenditure, which, even on the peace efta-blifhment (if poor-rates be included), already exceeds the grofs amount of all the landlords' rents in England :—a tax on the funds, of which the Dutch have long ago fet us the ex-ample, may therefore be expected, and may at laft roufe the monied men from that blind and felfifh acquiefcence in the meafures of every adminiftration, which has been the chief fupport of our war-politics.—A friend, Sir, to the family on the throne, to our limited monarchy, and our conftitution of three eftates—a friend, above all, to the interefts of my country, and the happinefs of the human race, I deprecate the continuance of this dreadful war—My reafons are now before you and the public—However ineffectual my humble exertions may be to ward off the impending calamities, I fhall ftill have the fatisfaction of having performed my duty, and can appeal to the Searcher of Hearts for the purity of my views.

, God of peace and love, look down in mercy on thy erring creatures! and bid hatred, madnefs, and murder ceafe !

July 25, 1793.

J. W.